Molly & CORRY

Digital

D-Day

This is a work of fiction. Names, characters, places and incidents either are the product of the author's imagination or, if real, are used fictitiously.

Nitere Publishing: ISBN 978-0-9956568-4-0

www.mollyandcorry.com

Dedicated to all of the readers who told me they loved Molly and Corry and demanded another one be written.

Let me know if you like it.

Enjoy reading!

Molly and Corry Titles:

Boot Up! The Friendship Paradox

Satellite Sleuths

Smash and Grab

Digital D-Day

MCDD_IS_AC3

Chapters

Mind Games

"Okay Mum," Molly shouted, as she leapt up the stairs to her room three steps at a time. She hadn't really heard her mum's request to sort out her swimming costumes and wasn't really bothered about anything, except the great new game she'd started last night. All the kids were playing it and for once Molly was in at the start.

"You should set out your swimming gear," advised Corry. Molly leapt across the bottom corner of her bed and slid into her cupboard, smoothly activating her computer as the chair rotated into position. Normally Corry, the world greatest Artificial Intelligence and Molly's best friend, would have done this for her before she entered her room, but Molly seemed a little too eager to play and after ignoring her Mum, well... Corry 'felt' Molly shouldn't be encouraged to act this way. Corry's world was uncomplicated by things like excitement.

"I'll do it later." Molly shrugged off Corry's advice and began the game. As a tall elfin warrior princess, Molly felt proud and confident in her role playing. The blue skin wasn't an issue, neither were the pointed ears or tattered dress. Within the game Molly was able to hold her own against anyone up to her level and her confidence was riding high.

"I don't understand the purpose of the activity," declared Corry, but Molly was wrapped up in a skirmish with two small furry creatures hissing and baring their teeth at her. She ignored her friend's request for information.

The headset covered her ears and the small microphone on the bendy stalk allowed her to talk to her companions within the game, but Corry's direct link through the device in Molly's ear could not be silenced. Having an artificial intelligence in your head was not always easy.

Corry noted Molly's rigid stance and excessive brain function, along with the tension in her right hand as she controlled, with superb accuracy the four-button mouse to manipulate the on-screen avatar.

"Mum's coming," warned Corry. Molly had been entranced for twenty minutes, but it seemed like only a few seconds to her.

"What for?" asked Molly, reluctant to suspend belief in her virtual world.

"She wants your swimming costumes," replied Corry.

"How do you know?" queried Molly, slashing once more at a purple crab-like creature nipping at her ankles from the oozing pink mud.

"She asked you when you arrived home and I reminded you when you sat at the game twenty-three minutes ago." Corry watched through the secret camera badge on Molly's jumper as the screen flashed red and Molly took a hit from a second crab creature emerging from the ooze beneath her feet.

Molly's hand flashed out and the game was paused. A countdown began in the centre of the screen. Pausing was only allowed for a maximum of two minutes. As she raised herself from her chair, Molly felt the stiffness in her back and winced. She left the cupboard and went across to her drawers lifting out two swimming costumes, noticing the ache in her right wrist as she did so. Both swimming costumes had been bought as part of her school uniform and were a dull dark blue. She idly wondered if she'd ever get the chance to wear something more colourful and fashionable like the people she'd seen on telly and in the holiday brochures.

"Got them then?" Mum announced herself as she entered Molly's room with a light tap on the door. Molly noticed the counter was down to forty-five seconds.

"Here you are," she almost threw the costumes at mum and rushed back to her seat. Mum was a little shocked by the abrupt treatment. Molly had returned to her chair in the cupboard and was replacing her headset, mentally transporting herself back into the avatar of Princess Molvarian Elfette, a name she'd conjured up herself. The counter reached ten and Mum was still in the room.

"How was your day, love? Are you looking forward to our holiday?" she asked. Molly gazed sternly at her mother.

"Sorry mum," she didn't sound sorry, "but I've got a world to save." The counter ran out, the world burst into life and in her mind Princess Molvarian Elfette had no time to chat to her mum.

After defeating the crab creatures, Molly cast a healing spell and recovered from her injuries. She checked her inventory and noticed a small gold throwing star had been added to her arsenal of weapons. She didn't hear her mum leave.

"That was quite rude, Molly." Corry was astonished at the way Molly had treated her mum. "What is it about that game?"

"I don't know!" Now the action was over Molly sounded contrite, "...but the counter was about to run out and..." her words trailed off. Thinking about her behaviour Molly was at a loss.

"Can you stop now?" asked Corry. "I hear dad's car approaching." Molly examined the virtual environment for threats and found none. She sat behind a large virtual boulder and cast a spell of invisibility. She then saved and left the game, reluctantly turning it off. She knew the game continued even when she wasn't there, but her invisibility would last up to twenty-four real hours and she should be safe. If you were discovered and killed you had to start again with no weapons or armour and that had been hard for Molly the first three times. She was adamant she wouldn't have to do that again.

Molly stood and stretched, she quickly changed out of her school uniform and into her jeans and tee-shirt. She glanced outside. The evenings were lighter and a little warmer as spring grew old and looked to summer to finish painting the gardens. She figured she didn't need her cardigan so removed the camera badge from her school jumper and pinned it to her tee-shirt.

"I'm home!" dad's shout came from the hallway. As usual he sounded happy, and Molly walked downstairs to supply his hug and 'welcome home' kiss, all the time thinking of her virtual world, the adventures and perils of Princess Molvarian Elfette.

"Just five more days Molly," dad enthused. Molly returned a wan smile. She wondered how she could protect her avatar for two whole weeks while she was away in Greece. "Why go on holiday now?" she moaned. "It's so inconvenient." Mum arrived and hugged dad and they both silently stared at Molly, who seemed to be staring at the wall in a daze.

"I'm looking forward to meeting the three-headed dog guarding all the zombies," laughed dad, teasing Molly about her previous adventures. He tried to provoke some reaction from his daughter, but she looked tired and distracted

"Cerberus, 1200 hit points, susceptible to Ice spells and Oak-Sap poison," muttered Molly, as she turned and walked into the kitchen without acknowledging her dads' wry comment.

"Is she kidding?" Dad sounded worried.

"It's that stupid game they're all playing." Mum sounded a little cross. "I think it might be taking away our little girl."

The holiday had been a big thank you gift from Georgios Saximo the famous Archaeologist and close friend of Lord James. James was an old pensioner who lived in the big house at the edge of town. He'd become acquainted with Molly when she'd found his missing parrot and since then the two of them had become really good friends, bonding over James' collection of exotic pets, which Molly often looked after. James told Molly he was retired and Molly knew he lived alone and was probably lonely, but all was not as it seemed. At the moment he was on holiday with Georgios, probably relaxing on a beach somewhere and Molly and her dad had been helping out by feeding his collection of strange pets.

Georgios, or George as his friends called him, had unearthed Molly's accidental discovery of Viking treasure a few months back and realised one of his lifelong ambitions in the process, for which he had become eternally grateful to Molly.

Molly and her family, older brother Tommy, who was currently out on his moped delivering pizzas and her younger brother, the toddling menace, Winston, had never been abroad on holiday and the whole house was buzzing with excitement over their upcoming trip to Greece.

"There are lots of ancient ruins to explore," dad tried to engage Molly in the real world as they ate their dinner. "Temples and shrines and huge theatres and gymnasiums all going back thousands of years, with statues and carvings of gods and heroes; who knows what we'll find?"

"Then there's the beaches and the cities to explore," added mum, just as excited as dad, but focussed on the present not the past.

Winston giggled loudly causing Molly to glance over at the gravy covered face beaming with mischief. 'Swamp sprite, level four, possible poison attack,' she thought.

"George has given us tickets for a three-day cruise on the Med, while we're there." Dad's excitement was getting the better of him. Molly had finished her dinner yet dad's plate was still full and getting cold. "It'll take us to Crete, Molly, where they say the original Labyrinth of the Minotaur was and we can go to Knossos where the king ordered Daedalus to build the maze to trap the creature and..."

Molly had glazed over again, her thoughts not really her own as the numbers and tactics whirled around inside her mind. 'Minotaur, level eighteen, susceptible to Spear of Light and additional ten hit points from any magic sword; map of the maze cost two hundred gold or available as a reward for Swamp Dragon quest, level twenty-two'.

"...made the wings for his son, Icarus." Dad looked at Molly in dismay, disappointed by her subdued reaction.

"It'll be fine when we get there," offered mum. She launched a pre-emptive strike on Winston's loaded spoon, removing the potential splat missile. "She's obviously had a hard day."

**

The shallow puddles on the pavement and around the school yard were the only evidence of last night's brief squally weather. Corry had woken Molly from her deep slumber and noticed how sluggish Molly was throughout her morning routine. A quick health analysis showed Corry that Molly had not gained much benefit from her sleep.

"The Health Minister advises that you need to stop playing your game at least an hour before you go to bed, Molly." Her concern for Molly was obvious in her voice. She'd already had to shout warnings twice; first as Molly attempted to cross the road without noticing a cyclist then, just when she thought they'd arrived safely, Molly stepped off the pavement in front of a small motorcycle with 'L' plates and a nervous rider, who wobbled as he tried to avoid her and nearly fell off. Corry's shout made Molly check her step back from the road and skip to safety. Corry was relieved when Molly finally stepped safely through the open iron gates and into the protection of the school.

It was strange how Molly thought of Corry as a she. It was obvious to her that Corry was simply a computer, she never claimed to be anything else, but Molly was convinced there was something unique that made Corry act like a living person; she just had a different type of body.

"I'm fine," claimed Molly, as she stifled a yawn behind her hand, ignoring the potential disasters she'd just narrowly avoided. The tired eleven-year-old made her way across the yard to her classmates and quietly stood beside Jasmine and Ezzy.

"No! Magic is much better." Ezzy was almost shouting at Jasmine. "Your strength is pointless if I stun you or paralyze you."

"...but, I can carry more and take more treasure," Jasmine was trying to be reasonable, "and I get to wear better armour when I get to a higher level and that'll make your magic useless against me." Jasmine was perplexed. In her mind the idea of magical protection was flimsy and unreal. A strong girl with a granite sense of right and wrong, Jasmine was feared by all of the school bullies, but to Molly she was a close supportive friend.

Jasmine had her own problems at home and these had threatened to overwhelm and isolate her, until Molly had braved her own fears and talked to the big girl sat all alone. She simply showed Jasmine respect and kindness, even though all the other kids thought their unkind thoughts and let their fears guide their prejudice. They all warned Molly to keep away from her, but Molly saw something else, she noticed a mask to hide a deep fear and Molly decided to help. She was glad she did.

Lizzie sidled up behind Molly. "I got on last night," she whispered. Lizzie was Molly's best human friend, they often worked together and achieved the highest marks in science, but Lizzie had a strange relationship with gadgets and computers. She believed that they all worked better if they were pink and sparkly. Lizzie's philosophy was that challenges such as turning the power on and updating your apps were things that could be confusing, but that was okay, that was what the help-desk was for. "Mum helped me," she needlessly explained.

"What are you?" asked Molly gruffly, trying to follow Jasmine's argument. Her tiredness turned to impatience when Lizzie's lack of common sense was put on show.

"I'm a princess," she replied, grinning.

"Okay, but what race are you?" Molly persisted, but there was an edge of contempt in her voice, amplified by her lack of rest and Lizzie retreated a little.

"I think, er, I'm not sort of in any races. I just picked some flowers and fruit and..." Lizzie wasn't sure about Molly's query and wondered why she was being shouted at by her friend.

"Human? Elf? Troll? What are you?" Molly's patience was wearing thin and her voice increased in volume as if that would make it clearer for Lizzie to understand.

"Human.... I think," stammered Lizzie, wondering if she'd done something wrong. "Mum set me up and...." Molly had refocused her attention and was now watching Ezzy.

"I'm up to level twelve already," she boasted to the ring of friends surrounding her. Molly's lip curled as she watched Ezzy crow about her achievement. The bell rung out, loud and piercing, threatening their ear drums while beckoning them into class.

"Another half an hour and I'd be level twelve too," she accused Corry as her friends scampered ahead of her. Corry had advised Molly when it was her bedtime, when it was an hour past her bedtime and then threatened to disconnect the game from the network, two and a half hours after her bedtime, in order to get Molly away from the screen. Corry had done quite a lot of research and while she understood the benefits of the game, she also recognised the symptoms of addictive behaviour.

"You'll get there tonight," whispered Corry in Molly's ear. Molly harrumphed.

"And where will Ezzy get to?" Molly moaned, watching her new nemesis enter the class ahead of her.

A hand grabbed her arm and Molly turned in shock and anger, her free hand balling into a fist, instantly prepared to attack and scream at her assailant, but her body ceased its struggle and she immediately relaxed when she recognised Stevie.

"Can't stop! Paladin, Silver Avenger; meet me at the Dancing Duck tonight around seven." With that he flashed his beautiful smile and strode off quickly down the corridor.

"A date?" whispered Molly watching her tall handsome friend dodge gracefully between the smaller bodies in the corridor and disappear around the corner.

"Not a real date. The Dancing Duck is a location in your game," clarified Corry.

"Okay then, it's a... digital date." For the first time in days Molly smiled and the tense frustration built up over days hunched over the computer, seeped from her body. A sudden wave of guilt shocked her. How unfair she'd been to Lizzie. A pang of regret kick-started a thought that she needed to apologise to her friend, but how?

"Corry?" she asked in a strange sweet innocent voice. "Can you link the school computers to the game?"

The Dancing Duck

The day was mundane, the lessons hardly challenging and if it wasn't for Corry, Molly would probably have fallen asleep. Maths was easy and now Geography, the last lesson of the day, was mega-boring. Mr Adamski loved his subject, but taught it as though there was no one in the room. He knew his stuff and information poured out into the silence, but he never connected with the students.

"Sir!" Molly was surprised by a loud voice at the rear of the class as it interrupted Mr Adamski's monologue on irrigation.

"Yes?" he quickly consulted his seating plan and concluded lamely "Esmerelda?"

"Sir, are crystals magical?" Ezzy was always trying to get teachers to support her theories that magic was real. She'd told everyone she'd been raised in the jungles of India until she was six and that she had witnessed mystical rituals and strange powers and, by association, believed she had them too. Molly rolled her eyes and tutted, others in the class shuffled around and paid attention to what was being said for the first time. Ezzy was the queen of distraction and occasionally she was quite humorous, but usually Molly just wished she'd shut up and listen.

"Well," began Mr Adamski, and to everyone's surprise he didn't tell Ezzy off. Instead he began talking about how crystals reacted when energy was put into them and how they could produce energy when put under pressure. He talked about crystal caves which generated super heat and crystal lasers turning flashing light into welding torches and for the first time Molly found him fascinating.

"We use crystals for precise timing too. Every computer works because the timing pulse from a crystal is so precise. But whether these properties are magic..." he sighed. "I suppose that depends on what you think magic is?"

On cue the bell rang. Mr Adamski closed his books. Without another word he shut down the projector and picked up his briefcase. Molly looked at Ezzy who was staring, with her mouth open, at the first teacher to contribute something positive to her view of the world.

"Ha! You fancy Adamski!" shouted Riley, he kicked Ezzy's desk and ran.

"It's all true Molly," Corry had listened to Mr Adamski's response to Ezzy. I use crystal timers all over the world to keep everything synchronised, without them I couldn't keep my networks communicating."

"But is it magic?" whispered Molly, aware there were still stragglers in the class.

"There are many quotes from scientists about magic, but essentially Arthur C Clark said 'any sufficiently advanced technology is indistinguishable from magic,' and he built satellites for a living and wrote books about space and weird mysterious things."

"Is he right?" Molly asked, slinging her bag over her shoulder.

"By definition, magical entities can create images; they know secret things and can foretell the future. If that is magic, I must be a sorcerer."

"Don't be silly," Molly laughed, drawing glances from a couple of students ahead of her. "I have sent a map to your phone showing tomorrows weather." Corry made a strange sound that sounded like an elephant coughing.

"Are you laughing?" Molly asked quietly as she left the class and entered the almost empty corridor. She pulled out her buzzing phone and viewed the image from Corry. "What's this big red number "10" in the corner?"

"That is Ezzy's real level, but shush, it's a secret," and once again Corry laughed.

***

As they entered their street, Corry reminded Molly of how rude she'd been to her mum the previous day and suggested she made up for it with a big hug before going upstairs to play on her game.

"Hi mum," Molly entered the kitchen and smiled at a sleeping Winston, still tied to his high chair.

"Seemed such a shame to move him," mum explained.

Molly hugged her mum. "What's that for?" mum was overjoyed, but slightly suspicious.

"I'm sorry I was a pain yesterday," Molly gave a smile "I was just caught up in that dumb game, it's all everyone talks about." She moved to the fridge and retrieved the milk, pouring herself a generous drink.

"Does that mean you'll give it a rest?" asked mum hopefully.

"Can't do that! Meeting Stevie tonight and we're going to team up." With that the fervour reappeared and Molly headed to her cupboard. Mum watched her go, smiled and shook her head.

***

The Dancing Duck was in a large town quite a distance away from Princess Molvarian's rock and Molly had to ask Corry for directions. Corry dutifully accessed the game data server and produced a map for Molly to follow. Molly didn't think of it as cheating, it was just making up for the lack of signposts on the road. To distance herself from further accusations she also ran away from creatures that sought to get in her way. She could easily have beaten them, she reasoned, but this way she wasn't gaining anything by using the ill-gotten map.

Corry had been intrigued by the game structure and was examining the program code; she thought it was very interesting.

On entering the inn, Molly noticed there was a distinct difference about the characters inside. Each had their avatar's name floating above their head. This was a chat room where any player could interact, ask for help, arrange deals for weapons and equipment ...and there was Stevie.

"...and the best bit is you can stay here as long as you want and you're kept safe." Stevie seemed to know everything about the game.

"I thought if we all got together and went around as a group we can register as a fellowship and get more points for our skills. Then we can take on some of the more rewarding quests and maybe even go after the Annihilator. What do you think?" Stevie was asking Molly for help, she didn't know what an Annihilator was, but there was no way she would let him down.

As they talked, other avatars approached the table and sat with the gleaming silver knight and the radiant blue skinned elf.

"Is that you Molly?" asked a tall muscular Amazonian warrior dressed in what looked like a swimming costume and a short leather skirt. "Molvarian, that's Molly isn't it? It's me, Jasmine."

"Hi Jazzy, glad you could come." Stevie greeted her and the three of them giggled.

"You look great Jasmine," Molly liked the warrior avatar, capable yet feminine, the name 'Xenaminar' hovered above her head.

"You look ... blue," laughed Jasmine "Who else is coming?"

"I spoke to you two, but I also put a coded message on the notice board at school, I'm not sure who else will turn up." Stevie explained. "I got an e-mail from the local server manager. He says if we form a local group we qualify for rewards. All we have to do is sign up. I'll send you the link." Moments later Molly's computer pinged.

"I mentioned it in Geography to Jaimie," Jasmine confessed. Molly smiled at the news, she liked Jaimie and Jerry. If one turned up so would the other. The two girls were inseparable.

The door to the Dancing Duck flew open and a large blue shimmering sphere appeared. Inside a smaller dark figure materialised. Molly knew who it was from the moment she saw the pointed black hat.

"Hi Stevie, it's me Ezzy." The name above the witchy avatar was simply 'Esmerelda'.

"That's just your name," laughed Molly, the others chuckled.

Ezzy sounded a little angry as she announced, "I am Sister Esmerelda of the Coven of the Dark Blood Moon! I happen to think Esmerelda is a very good name for a witch!" and with that the laughter stopped.

The door opened one final time and a small blue and silver robed battle-dwarf carrying a huge ornate war-hammer entered. The grizzled old face surveyed the gathered avatars, but did not approach their table.

"Okay," called Stevie, bringing them all to attention. "This will be our base for now. If anything happens to anyone we meet back here. Agreed?" They all agreed. "I suggest we take on the small bandit gang at the edge of town, there's three of them, and we can claim the reward from the Guardhouse. As a Paladin I get better rewards for doing 'Good' deeds. Is there anyone here who needs to do 'Evil' stuff?" They all murmured in assent claiming their heroic credentials aligned to 'Good' then slowly they all turned to look at Ezzy.

"No," Ezzy defended herself. "I'm aligned to 'Chaos'. I can do 'Good' or 'Evil' stuff. It doesn't matter to me."

***

In a dark basement lit only by the light from six monitors, two displaying the virtual world of Molly's game and four showing coloured coded strings of alphanumeric characters steadily scrolling up the screen, a dark hunched figure observed the chat taking place in the Dancing Duck. The figure, dressed all in black, mumbled as his agile fingers caressed the keyboard on his lap. His wide leather office chair swung as he jostled to the right and retrieved his drinks can from a small side table. The sweet syrup flowed down his throat and he smacked his lips sighing loudly. His almost black irises closed tighter, as the blue sphere materialised, brightening his central screen too much for comfort.

"That's four," he crowed. "One more, one more, come on." He urged the screen to comply. Two more characters entered together and joined the group just as the witch stopped shouting. Two Norse warriors walked to the table, one male, one female, almost twins to look at wearing similar style armour and the same blonde hairstyle. Jaimie and Jerry announced their identities. "Six! Brilliant that's a bonus for me." The dark hunched figure bounced a little in his anticipation. "They'll definitely take me on now," he whispered.

***

"Molly I have a concern regarding your game," announced Corry as the new troop agreed to follow Stevie on their first quest.

Molly muted her microphone. "I know, I know, it's bad for me and I need my sleep and it's addictive and you think...," she moaned, repeating the repertoire she'd heard twenty times before.

"No, I mean, yes, but that is not my immediate concern." Corry sounded almost flustered.

"Molly the location of the game origin is hidden. Why would anyone hide their network?"

"Probably to stop nosey computers looking at their private stuff," rebuked Molly.

"But Molly," Corry was aware of the argument the two had about privacy. As an AI, Corry always believed that data was as essential to her as air was to people, and no one should be allowed to stop other people breathing. Molly just thought Corry was nosey and couldn't stop herself from investigating other people's secrets.

"This is very advanced code. It uses the game to take your data then profile your reactions and decisions, it also builds on the data by searching through all of your internet communication and your digital profile on social media, it even records everything you say, but then it sends it somewhere I cannot locate. Why would anyone need so much information about you and your friends?"

"Maybe it's to work out real challenges in the game, maybe it sets up better communication between our 'fellowship', maybe it..." but Molly was suspicious now, all of these things were part of the game anyway, so why hide all that data? She thought hard for a moment then reluctantly asked Corry, "Is it safe?"

"I detect no adverse effects on our system; it seems to take, not deliver, data. I'll perform a full backup for safety, but at the moment it's just suspicious activity not malicious code. I'll see what I can find." With that Corry went silent.

While the chat was proceeding in the Dancing Duck, Molly was trying her best to maintain a distance between Ezzy and Stevie. The little gowned witch dressed in black, complete with crooked pointy hat and black fingernails didn't look appealing to Molly, but Molly also knew her blue skinned Elf was not everyone's cup of tea. Molly was jealous of the attention Stevie was paying to the others.

As the evening wore on someone else began to get jealous too, though if you asked them to define their feelings, they probably couldn't.

Corry decided to join the game.

Terence

"Have you put those bins out yet?" the muffled shout was clear to Terence, sat in his dark, dingy room below the house.

"Doing it!" he yelled back and placed his keyboard neatly on the table in front of him, swivelled his chair and stood. He approached the stairs to the house and as he ascended, the door above opened and his Gran stood there, arms folded across her chest.

"Wasting your time down here again!" she accused. "What's wrong with you?" she shrilled.

Terence didn't flinch as he passed her in the doorway though he knew the slap would land heavily across the back of his head. Instead he mumbled and apologised for his life and stepped away quickly to deal with the household chores.

"You're useless, just like your dad was." Gran had never had time for Terence's dad. He'd died in an accident while working abroad and had the audacity to abandon his family.

Terence was young when his dad died and never really knew him, but his mum provided a stable home to raise him. He was happy for about two years... and then she died in a car accident.

"I should have left you to rot in that home. You're just a burden to me." His Gran screamed. The hostility in her voice always made Terence feel strange, both angry and sad, a tear welled up in his eye, but his anger kept it from rolling down his cheek. Then the doubt and guilt would worm its way into his head. He knew he wasn't an upstanding citizen; he knew he didn't have a regular job; he knew he had no real friends, no-one he could call, no one who would care. He knew his life was worthless, he'd heard it so many times.

"If it wasn't for me and your granddad you'd have starved by now." Without thinking he ducked and the slap from his pursuing Gran failed to land, infuriating her. She screamed her anger and punched him, her bony fist digging into his back adding another bruise to the collection he carried.

At the age of eleven, Terence had been processed as an orphan and placed in care, not fully understanding why. His life became a struggle to survive. Not everyone in the care home was there through bad luck... some had earned their place.

When his Mum's dad had died, a Granddad he had never seen, his Grandma requested Terence be released into her care. Terence knew she was family so agreed. He never questioned why he'd been left aside for so long.

In care for four years before his Gran showed an interest, he'd laid in his bed at the home, imagining her joy as his existence had been revealed, imagining her delight at being reunited with her own flesh and blood. He even imagined her tears of happiness as they hugged for the first time.

She'd collected him without a word, smiling and fawning to the suited officers checking the paperwork. Terence sat with everything he owned in a beat-up grey holdall with a broken zip. He thought her smiles just made her look sad.

Over the first two days his new situation was made clear to him. He was there to be at her beck and call, to carry out the menial tasks she didn't want to do. To cook and clean, fetch and carry, and in return he could sleep in his room and eat regularly. He was her servant not her grandson. Any joy, any happiness remained firmly in his imagination.

He had never known praise from her and her acceptance of him was a daily battle. She enjoyed taking her anger out on him and sometimes she would drink a little too much and rail at him, blaming the world for all of her problems; blaming his father for the loss of her daughter, blaming her husband for deserting her, dying without her permission. Blaming Terence for destroying her family, blaming everyone, but herself, for the life she led. He understood her pain, he understood her loss, after all he shared it. No matter how he tried he couldn't understand why he was to blame and the doubt burned into his soul.

Terence enjoyed school as a respite from his daily life and excelled in maths and computers. The school close to his Gran's had accepted him at a late age after examining his life-story. He attended with an open mind, willing to make friends and fit in, but his skills in maths set him apart and his classmates had had four years to bond without him. They didn't see why that should change. Jealousy, fear of being replaced in the hierarchy and simple ignorance meant he was socially shunned. He told himself he didn't care and threw his efforts into his studies.

He had a great teacher who taught him to code, "You're way ahead of the curve," he'd been told and one day after class the teacher spoke to him, "I'm looking for someone to start a Computer club, how about it?" The club was a roaring success. Over time he won awards for his coding and learned all about hardware. Terence gathered spare parts from old computers at school and built his first very own computer. The teacher was so proud he'd taken a photo and printed it in the school newspaper. He was given the software he needed as a reward and was allowed to take his creation home.

"You ain't using that in here!" declared his Gran, "I can't afford all that electricity."

"It's the schools," he'd lied, "I have to work on it, and it doesn't take much power." Slowly, she stopped complaining about the computer, but on seeing the accumulation of papers and devices around it and his joy his work when he used it, she simply decided to ban it from his bedroom.

He moved into the basement three weeks later, after his Gran had slapped him and threatened him with the loss of his bedroom for being 'dirty' and 'lazy'. He'd already decided the bedroom wasn't suitable for his plans and for the first time Terence took the opportunity to move into the bigger room with space for his growing number of rescued computers. Pretending to be angry he blamed his Gran. "So now I have to sleep in the cold damp cellar," he shouted and slammed the door to punctuate his pretence of anger over the move, manipulating her the way she'd manipulated him for years. She wouldn't feel bad for him, if she thought he was being punished; she'd leave him alone.

By the time he'd finished college Terence had a powerful network of old machines and the ability to make money from his coding skills, but as is often the way his unguided journey towards riches had led him down a dark path. Terence became a hacker. He used his skills to steal and sell data, he scammed people by sending out phishing messages and last year he'd joined an anonymous group on the Internet that elevated him to ransom-ware. They had servers all around the world and Terence could launch his attacks with a small amount of protection. He knew everything could be traced eventually, but he also knew that making it difficult to find him would persuade the authorities to give up their chase. It simply wasn't worth the time and effort.

He would infect important computers, lock up their data and demand money to release it. He'd threaten to delete it or even worse, threaten to publish it for everyone to see. By focussing on big businesses, the group were making big money. By acting together, they remained hidden.

He felt no remorse; he knew he wasn't good enough to fit in with 'normal' society. He'd been told so many times, it had to be true. What else could he do?

The day Terence received an email detailing all of the ransom demands he'd made locked his life onto the path it now followed. It was not the police, but an organised gang of criminals who were impressed by his abilities. "Work for us or we send these details to interested parties", they threatened him.

Terence was smart enough to realise he could end up in jail and never be able to go online again. The jail time didn't worry him, he'd felt imprisoned most of his life anyway, but he didn't want to lose his meagre stolen wealth and knew he couldn't survive without access online for the rest of his life. The criminals recruited him to work for them and sweetened the deal with more money and better equipment. They were the people who'd provided him with the setup he now enjoyed: the racks of spare equipment lining each wall and the high-power systems running quietly in the corner. They'd also provided him with the control codes of the game all the kids were enjoying.

All they wanted him to do was gather the players together and relay the group data collected. Simple and lucrative, who cares what the big crime lords did with all that data.

He'd been promised a new hacking tool by the gang and a new way to increase his wealth, if he could only generate a certain amount of data subjects. Now, Stevie and Molly had pulled their band of adventurers together, these would meet the quota; he'd finally receive his reward.

But first, he'd have his fun. He'd taken all their details, now he didn't need them in the game. He logged into the virtual world and became "The Annihilator".

***

"Level fifteen already. Well done Molly." Stevie praised her efforts and she began to colour up, a little embarrassed, even though he couldn't actually see her in her cupboard, while playing the game in his home. "That was great the way you levitated him and disarmed him. I didn't have much to do to dispatch him at all."

"Another dead troll, another safe bridge," she chuckled as she cast healing spells on Jaimie and Jerry. Jasmine was unhurt and Ezzy wasn't with them, it was a great session.

"And now you face me," a rumbling deep voice assailed the adventurers. A deep blue haze appeared and through it walked a large black-armoured knight with glowing purple eyes. Unlike Stevie's the armour did not shine.

"Looks like an evil Paladin," remarked Stevie, calmly. "Places everyone, Jasmine first, Molly give her a shield."

"I am the Annihilator," boasted Terence, "I don't need you anymore. Prepare to die." What followed seemed to defy the rules of the game. The evil knight was hit from all sides yet suffered no damage. He pointed at Jaimie and she was instantly encased in a block of ice.

Luckily just as she was hit, Molly had cast a healing boost spell and this prevented Jaimie from instant death.

"You can't do that," the Annihilator was angry, his first kill had failed. Jasmine attacked him with a spear and though it was hanging out of the character on the screen, he again suffered no damage.

Stevie had manoeuvred stealthily behind the evil knight and used his Paladin strength, plus his "Might of Right" attack, which should have destroyed anything up to level one hundred and fifty, yet still the Annihilator showed no damage.

"It's a cheat," yelled Stevie and all of the players took instant screen shots to record the incident.

"It doesn't matter, you'll all be dead in a few seconds and people will say it's just sour grapes. Ha!" Terence spun to face his attacker, but Stevie had jumped away, instead his gaze rested on a willowy blue elf.

Molly stared as the evil knight's weapon began to glow green, her screen flashed blue and for a second went black. "Am I dead?" she whispered.

The monitor cleared and the full troop had joined Ezzy, sat around the table in the Dancing Duck.

"But how?" asked Stevie, totally perplexed. "Was that you Molly?"

A small glowing yellow dot, settled on the table, the name above was taller than the avatar and read, 'Red Scarf (Fairy).'

Molly looked really close at her monitor and could just make out a tiny transparent fairy wearing a thin red scarf.

A small voice squeaked in a high pitch, "I have no defence and only a little life, but lots of magic and no-one can see me." The troop was amazed, none of them were aware of this class of character, and who would choose to be so fragile, so intangible. "May I join your group?" it asked in its tinny little voice.

"Do we know you?" asked Jasmine.

"No, I have never met you before and only joined the game a few minutes ago, I am alone. The fight back there just didn't seem fair. Isn't that what Fairies are for, to make things fairer?"

"Welcome," laughed Stevie. "Welcome and our thanks to the mighty Red Scarf Fairy."

Power Play

"It's you, isn't it?" Molly accused Corry while she was brushing her teeth the next morning.

"Pardon, Molly? What is me?" asked Corry in the most innocent voice Molly had ever heard.

"That Fairy! The Red Scarf one, that's you. Admit it!" Molly had spent a great deal of time thinking about how the team had been rescued and what it had said about itself. "Did you join the game?"

Corry was uncomfortable. She hadn't done anything wrong. She hadn't lied to anyone or cheated in any way. Admittedly her reflexes were about a million times faster than any other player, but she had deliberately sought to make things equal by reducing her defences. Yet now she felt awkward admitting what she'd done. It was as if her morality code had said she was doing something naughty, but she couldn't find out what.

"I know it's you!" accused Molly again, but then she laughed. "Only you would name yourself after an item of clothing and miss the point entirely."

"What do you mean?" asked Corry, now feeling insulted.

"Well, people call themselves after their appearance all the time, like Stevie is the 'SILVER' Avenger, but that's because he has special silver armour and that's very rare in the game. And that strange wolf-girl who calls herself the Baldric Bandit, that's because her main weapons are her throwing knives and they're held in her Baldric, that belt over her shoulder." Molly laughed again, "But no-one would name themselves after a useless red scarf that can't even be seen."

"I needed a name and something that identified me, so you can tell me from other fairies," explained Corry. "There were no slots for clothing or armour so I..." Corry paused.

"What did you do?" asked Molly, intrigued and a little worried.

"I just, slightly changed the character to let it wear a scarf or a hat. There had to be a way to change the appearance so that my character could be an individual." Corry was a little more positive now that she'd logically determined the reason for her action. She hoped Molly would understand.

"Does that mean you can cheat? You can change the code?" asked Molly, thinking evil thoughts that included Ezzy falling back to level 1, wearing yellow wellies, gym shorts and a rainbow bobble-hat next time they met.

"No. I can only access the characters database; I can't access the code unless I crack some very complex security and you said I should not do that. Anyway, cheating is wrong." Corry was confident again and her voice was emboldened.

"Why haven't we seen any fairies before? I don't remember being offered the chance to be one." This had also worried Molly. She preferred magic to fighting and she liked the idea of being sneaky and invisible, so she'd joined as a 'Rogue', a shadowy elf that could use lots of magic and become invisible later in the game. "If I'd have seen what Fairies could do, I'd be one too."

"It was an old character class that was marked as 'retired', but there have been Fairies in the game, I checked," claimed Corry, and Molly wouldn't think to question her, Corry loved checking out digital things. She couldn't possibly find a database without analysing all the data, old and new. In fact, Molly was so fed up with Corry's data investigations she'd been forced to give firm instructions that in future, Corry was not to tell her about the data she'd analysed whenever they watched anything on TV. Corry always checked out the systems that were used for things like studio special-effects and was always ruining the suspense for Molly by suddenly announcing why the exploding helicopter couldn't hurt anyone, because it wasn't really there, or the person talking to the monster was safe, because they were filmed in a different studio. Presented with the opportunity to access data, Corry was 'like a kid in a candy store', as dad always said; but she was never wrong.

"Okay, but don't tell anyone who you really are, and try not to do super-stuff until someone asks you." Molly laid down the law and Corry agreed.

***

"I don't believe it! There are no Fairies!" yelled Terence at the screen in front of him. "Fairies don't exist." He laughed quite crazily, remembering the line from the Peter Pan film he'd illegally downloaded. He thought quietly for a moment then furiously went to work on his keyboard.

"Gotcha!" Terence located the changes Corry had made in the game. The Fairy was a device for a game-tester. It was a cheat-character used by testers to examine the game, so they would not be killed while looking for bugs and glitches. Fairies could instantly run away to any part of the game. They were also so small that the testers could continue to monitor what was going on without getting in the way of the players. Someone had re-activated the character, and he now knew who'd done it.

"The address of the computer is...," a string of numbers identifying Molly's computer, flashed on the screen. Terence chuckled evilly. "I see you." he cackled as Molly's computer's private details appeared on his screen.

***

There were a crowd of students and several parents stood just inside the gate as Molly approached her school. "What's happening?" she whispered to Corry.

Jasmine saw her and shouted "Power Cut! Looks like schools shut." A muted cheer rose from the students around her and angry parents were asking for explanations from a bemused Mr Adamski still in his overcoat. From the top of the steps leading to the main door Mrs Bridger, the Deputy Headmistress, materialised. She looked down her nose at the assembled bodies in the yard below, registering the parents as simply larger students.

"Several areas of the town have had their power turned off, Molly." Corry informed Molly of her investigation. "The Electricity Control program seems to have developed a fault."

"Attention!" Mrs Bridger spoke forcefully without raising her voice and a heavy silence crushed the crowd's concerns. "Due to a 'Power Failure'," Molly noticed how Mrs Bridger could voice her punctuation. "I have been 'advised', that under Health and Safety legislation the students should not be admitted for lessons. We have no heating or lighting and we have no emergency alarm systems, nor do we have any communication systems at this time." The adults began to murmur seeing the depth of the problems for the first time.

Stevie appeared beside Molly, "How's your power at home?" he asked.

"No problems when I left," she responded.

"Our home is not affected, Molly" supplied Corry. Molly rolled her eyes, more information she couldn't use. This was the biggest problem with Corry, she always told Molly things she shouldn't really know.

"The school will remain closed today, and we would ask you to check the website for further updates as information is received. Thank you." With that Mrs Bridger slid through the doorway, back into the school and the sound of the locks being engaged triggered the sound of the crowd. Mr Adamski ran up the steps, but couldn't get in.

Children cheered, parent's whinged and Stevie shouted to the troop, "See you in 'The Duck', one hour." Ezzy, Jaimie and Jerry all nodded and Molly noticed Riley was watching closely, staring at Jasmine.

"Are you playing?" asked Jasmine.

"Not much else to do," replied Molly.

"You have Maths homework and an English essay to complete for tomorrow, Molly." Corry helpfully reminded her.

"See you in an hour," smiled Molly, ignoring Corry.

***

The new computer hacking tool worked. Terence was very pleased with himself. He was planning his revenge on the hacker who'd dared to mess with his system when the e-mail arrived with the new program link. This was far more exciting.

The new program was easy to set up and Terence soon understood the way the system worked. He could point at any area of a network or even a location on a map to select a target. Security in any computer system he selected was overridden automatically, with a simple click of his mouse, though there was a short delay while access was obtained by his software using intuition, guesswork and finally brute force. Moments later he was presented with a graphical representation of the program areas successfully hacked. Pictures appeared accompanied by options for actions his system could perform.

Terence chose Molly's school and the nearby shops as his first target; he clicked and watched the area turn grey and then green as he gained control. Presented with an icon containing a lightning bolt over the green shape, he selected "Electrical Shutdown," from the options listed. He clicked and the shape turned red. It was the easiest option for him to physically check. Coloured images were one thing, but Terence had to know whether the program worked in real life.

A few minutes later he leaned against a lamppost watching the crowd inside the school gates and smiled at his handiwork.

"This is going to be fun," he chuckled, as angry and bewildered parents, along with their smiling offspring, left the schoolyard. Pulling up his jacket collar like a cool conman, he returned to his basement with a wide smile beaming across his face.

***

Molly returned to her home and apprised mum of the situation.

"It's all off," she said. "They've sent us home 'til it's fixed." Molly, by force of habit entered the kitchen and made a bee line for the fridge.

"What's off?" asked mum, stretching up into a wall cupboard, obviously searching for something.

"The power," replied Molly. She grabbed a glass from the shelf and poured herself a glass of milk, quickly skipping to her left to avoid Winston's grasping hand as he leaned over from his high chair to grab her. It was covered in slobber and damp biscuit, looking like some exotic skin disease, a bit like the zombies in her game.

"Well you can help me with Winston..." began mum.

"Sorry Mum, I've got homework," she shouted, as she ran up the stairs to her bedroom.

On hearing Molly's shout, Corry had started the computer and was a little dismayed as Molly, donned the headset and immediately began to play the game.

A signal blinked in Terence's basement as Molly's computer logged on to the game. "There you are! Let's see now, who are you?" he tapped his keyboard and watched as Molly's stored images began to appear on the screen in front of him. A list of Molly's school work appeared followed by Molly's emails. "A little girl!" He couldn't believe the system was showing him Molly's details. As the images scrolled on, he found a few pictures of Tommy, Molly's brother. "That's more like it," he sneered. He downloaded the full contents of Molly's computer and using the internet, found some personal details about Tommy.

Terence had a narrow view of the world and his limited exposure to people socially meant his view of the world was quite distorted. In his mind he was a hacker and he was a young man, therefore as Tommy was a young man, he must be the hacker.

While all this was going on, blissfully unaware of the intrusion, Molly and Corry were earning experience points by wiping out strange orange skinned zombies in an old mine.

"Behind you!" yelled Corry as a lumbering scarred pale orange figure staggered, arms outstretched towards Molly. Corry momentarily detected an excessive data upload, but there was no interruption to the computer, so she simply marked it for later investigation and focussed on the challenges Molly was facing. She urgently cast a protective barrier between Molly and two more pale creatures.

Blue fire sprang from Molly's short sword and the creatures fell, smouldered and vanished. "One more to go!" she yelled excitedly. As her avatar raced toward the last zombie, Molly changed her weapon, loading a fire-ball spell she'd recently learned. She let fly the flaming missile which hurtled towards the desiccated monster, depleting all of her magic in the process. Corry watched the beast quickly staggered to the right in an attempt to avoid the attack, but she targeted her own paralysis spell to hold it in place. The two watched as the final immobile creature burned, collapsed and faded from sight. "That was lucky," sighed Molly. "No magic left. Thanks." She acknowledged her friend's intervention; in the excitement she'd left herself defenceless.

"Ten minutes and we have to return to the inn," announced Corry.

"Can't you just teleport me?" asked Molly. She watched as her magic slowly returned.

"Yes, but do we want the others to think we are together?" Corry was aware that suspicious behaviour could lead to too many questions. She suspected Ezzy would make life difficult for both of them if Molly gave her any cause for concern.

"You're right," Molly retrieved a large purse of gold coins and a magical hooded cape from the treasure chest they'd liberated from the final zombie and together the friends returned to the town. Corry zipped ahead and materialised in the Dancing Duck while Molly walked the last few virtual streets alone, although a blue robed dwarf seemed to be following her.

Big Reward

Processing the roadside camera feed, Terence's computer system was watching for Tommy's moped. According to the college timetable his last lesson finished fifteen minutes ago and Tommy should be returning home soon. Terence had set the computer to watch for Tommy's number plate as it drove along the main road back to town. The first part of his revenge was taking shape. A screen showed Tommy's progress from multiple angles, feeding images to the system from all nearby cameras. Every time Tommy approached a traffic light, the new software immediately turned it to red, meaning the moped had to slow down and stop.

He'd practised turning things on and off all over the county. Power was easy, he'd even shutdown a factory. Traffic signals were fun, but a bit trickier. Feeling full of confidence from the power and control at his command, he laughed aloud at the idea of people sat on the toilet when the lights went out or missing the end of their programs on telly. This inconvenience really appealed to Terence's sense of humour. He was enjoying himself immensely. His favourite activity had become messing around with road signals where he could monitor the traffic through local cameras; it was his own private comedy show and he was beginning to feel a bit like an all-powerful sorcerer. It was magic.

"Ha! Take that!" he'd shout and point at the screen. The lights obeyed him and turned red. Every vehicle halted was a small victory. The trouble was Terence was still learning his new program and he ended up making all the lights turn to red at the same time. Very quickly the whole town became gridlocked; not a vehicle could move.

Tommy's bike puttered gently along the road home. Seeing the traffic problems ahead, Tommy pulled over, turned off his engine and dismounted his bike. He decided to push it home on the pavement. It was a lot quicker than dealing with the traffic jam.

"NO! NO! NO!" Terence watched through a security camera attached to a fast- food outlet, as Tommy strode off down the pavement gently wheeling his bike. Terence's anger was getting the better of him when a small chime indicated he had mail.

"Uh oh! It's them." His new hacking software showed him that the email had come from the same criminals. Terence wondered if he'd done something wrong. They'd never contacted him twice in the same month before, but now, twice in the same day. As he read the communication, he realised his employers had found something strange in the data from the little girl's computer.

"Isolate all references to files..." and a long list of folders and files appeared, each with names that made no sense. Strings of letters and numbers and strange symbols identified files no human had ever written.

"DELETE ALL, IMMEDIATELY!" The email was using capital letters... these instructions had been 'shouted'. Whatever it was must be bad, thought Terence. "DO NOT communicate with source device EVER!" he read.

This last instruction was too much for Terence. He was a bit miffed that they'd been watching the information he'd obtained from the little girls' computer and for a fleeting moment he panicked about some of the stuff he'd seen and done on the Internet. "They probably monitor everything." He whispered his thoughts to the dark room. "Whatever it is it must be important," his interest in Tommy was quickly forgotten.

Terence located the folders and saw the files. He highlighted them and was about to push 'Delete', but then his ego kicked in. "I thought you were the big bad guys," he mocked the message on the screen, then went to work and isolated the files listed. "I bet these are his hacking files." He whispered. Being curious he opened one of the folders, there were thousands of really small files in each folder, but instead of deleting the strange files, as he'd been warned, he fetched an empty external storage device from a rack of spare parts and moved them over. He planned to examine them and maybe learn eve more hacking secrets.

Using an old computer he had on the back shelf, he booted the operating system and made sure all networking, Wi-Fi, Bluetooth even the old Infra-Red was turned off and disabled. He visually double checked to ensure there were no network cables attached. As he worked, in his mind he built up an image of his adversary, equipped with superior hacking tools and wearing the face of Tommy.

"Now what is it that's got you guys so excited?" He'd convinced himself that the files were a more advanced hacking tool than his own. "Jealousy, that would explain it," he thought aloud, judging others by his own shortcomings.

"Who's that?" His Gran's angry voice came from the top of his stairs in the basement. "Have you got someone down there with you?" There was a loud bang on the door.

"It's just the radio," he smirked. He'd tried to explain the Internet and media feeds to her, but his Gran couldn't, or more likely wouldn't understand. Listening to a radio was such an old idea, he thought. The door was kicked again.

"Isn't it enough, that you've stuck me in here?" he sounded angry, but he was actually smiling. Gran muttered something about 'toenails' he couldn't quite hear and the door remained silent. "I'm never cutting those things again!" he called gently, not loud enough for her to hear. The image of his Gran's yellow and black toenails capping her twisted and bunion covered toes sent a shiver down his spine.

Focussing on the task in hand Terence connected the external drive to the USB port of the old computer. He checked the screen, listing the files and clicked to execute each of the application files displayed, one at a time. He was confident that the computer was isolated from everything else. Whatever this software was, he had it contained.

The third file he activated was the only one that showed any response. The screen went blank. For a moment Terence thought it might be a simple virus designed to delete all of the computer's files and wondered what all the fuss was about, but then a small tinny, warbling voice came from the ancient built-in speaker.

"Hello, my name is CORVUS."

World Gone Mad

For the last week dad's mood had been exceedingly happy. The countdown to the holiday was creating excitement that he could barely contain, but as he walked through the door this evening he was scowling. He slammed the door behind him. Mum hurried to hug him and find the cause of his anger.

"Are you okay love?" she asked with real concern.

"Everything's wrong and no-one knows what to do," he announced. He balled his fists and removed his jacket throwing it at the hook and watching it slide to the floor. His frustration was evident in every movement he made. He snatched at the jacket and missed; letting out a low roar he retrieved it on the second swipe.

Mum backed off, "I'm sure, it's not that bad," she said, as she dismissed her husband's bad mood and went to put the kettle on. "You'll feel better after a cuppa." Her mind was in turmoil, she had rarely seen her husband act like this, whatever it was it was unlikely to be 'nothing'.

Molly had heard dad come in and felt the wall shake as the door slammed shut. She'd parked her character in the inn for safety and left the game to investigate. Quietly, she crept down the stairs and took a seat in the room, unseen by dad. His zombified state didn't encourage a hug.

Corry was very concerned about dad. From Molly's camera badge she detected his high blood pressure and excessive muscular tension. "Dad needs to relax," she whispered.

They all sat in the front room and waited for dad to get comfortable in his chair before mum unwisely asked him, "How was your day then dear? "Dad sipped his hot tea and took a deep breath before responding. "All the traffic lights turned red on the way to work," he began.

"Is that all," mum laughed and stood as if the crisis was over and there was no more to be said. Tommy had mentioned the traffic delays when he came in, so mum knew there had been some road problems.

"No, that was annoying..., but it was every light, at the same time and that led me to call the council to ask why," dad continued. "The manager was quite co-operative and explained that their computers were 'acting weird'."

He took a deep breath and Molly saw him consciously relax his body, it sagged. "Did you know certain streets are losing power all over the county and no-one knows why?" Mum returned to her seat to listen, there was obviously more to dad's tale.

"There's no pattern, no mechanical faults. The only thing the areas have in common is that everything affected is controlled by computers; but no-one can find out what's happening." Dad sipped his tea again, staring ahead, unblinking. "Factories, schools and transport..." he announced.

"I think..." he paused and read the wallpaper again, staring hard at a point just beyond the end of his nose.

"I think..." he repeated quietly, "...if I didn't know better, I'd say it's an attack!"

Just Doing My Job

"Really?" George stared with dismay at James. "You sent a postcard?" He took a drink to quench his thirst and splashed his face to relieve the heat.

"Well, I was in character. What else do tourists do in Thailand?" James grinned at George's disbelieving face.

"We are here to find possibly the greatest fabled treasure of the age..." began George, pulling his sweat stained shirt away from his body and wafting the breeze beneath his damp armpits.

"I thought you found that with Molly, when she discovered Wulfen and his dagger." James teased his archaeologist friend as they made their way slowly into the dense jungle. It seemed to George that James didn't feel the heat at all; he showed barely a drop of sweat on his brow despite his advanced years.

The secret was simple; when James came out of retirement as a government agent, to help

Molly, all be it in only a part time capacity, he had been issued with many new gadgets by his new controller, Corvus. One of those gadgets was a thermal regulation suit and he was wearing it now, under his khaki shirt and trousers. The baking hot damp jungle heat was kept at bay while the suit was set to a cool sixteen degrees Celsius.

George hacked and slashed through the undergrowth creating a path to the site he had calculated, which lay just a few miles ahead. "Probably another four hours of this," he informed James.

James was busy inspecting a large yellow snake hanging from a branch above his head. He liked snakes, though didn't have many in his collection and anyway, this one was healthy, it didn't need saving. All of the exotic 'pets' back home had been rescued during one of James' adventures, except his parrot, Prospero; he was a family heirloom.

"So, we're looking for a magic flute," James conversed coolly.

George stopped hacking the foliage and bent over, breathing heavily. He turned his sweat drenched face to look at James and took a deep, unsatisfying damp breath, "Yes!" he managed between panting wheezes.

"Perhaps I could have a go," the old man offered. He retrieved a large half serrated, dull black bladed machete from his backpack. It made a quiet swishing noise as it brushed against its dull black scabbard. James looked at the blade and smiled. He adjusted his grip for comfort and hefted the blade once through the air. A low almost imperceptible buzz filled the air around the blade, but James wasn't tempted to hold it close to his ear to listen. He strode forward as George gratefully staggered back from the arm thick branch he'd been attacking. The sweat drenched archaeologist nodded in appreciation of his friends help, but secretly held no expectation of the old man advancing through the choked undergrowth.

"Like this?" James chuckled his query cheekily, fully aware of his friend's preconceptions. A glint of blue light sparkled along the edge of the blade as the tree before him was felled with what could only be described as a gentle sweep of his arm.

***

"...but sir, this is out of the ordinary, we should investigate." Dad tried his best to appeal to his boss, the General. He'd worried about the potential damage that could be caused by any system advanced enough to hack the main government computers and decided to see his boss as soon as he got to work.

"Civilian matter: Nothing to do with us. We can't get involved." It was as if the General didn't disagree with the sentiment, but understood there was a different way this should be handled. Dad was becoming agitated.

"They've hit power, schools, homes..." dad began again.

"Listen to me. Your computer is everything you said it was, but there are other people who do other things. You're not Superman. You can't save the world on your own." The General sighed and looked away from his friend. "All I can say is ...it's being handled," but he didn't sound convinced. "Leave it. Besides, I thought you were going on holiday?" the General brightened, trying to cheer dad up a little. "Two weeks in the sun?"

"Tomorrow night," but Molly's dad seemed to have lost his enthusiasm for the trip.

***

Molly heaved her new suitcase onto the bed.

"The plan is, I sit in the inn and the others will check on me from time to time," announced Molly.

"I can constantly monitor you and the game; I can even use your avatar..." offered Corry.

"No, you have to just play as you, so they don't suspect anything." Molly was adamant this ruse would create distance between her and Corry's characters and remove any suspicion from Ezzy's devious mind that the two of them were somehow working together. Molly's extra wealth and Corry's quick increase in level had made

Ezzy suspicious. She'd already asked in front of everyone in the class, if the two of them were real friends and were working together without the troop. The plan was set and for the first time Molly was starting to feel excited about the Mediterranean trip.

"Have you heard anything from Granddad recently," Molly was making small talk as she folded and packed her clothes in the case mum had provided for her. It had a yellow and black design all over it and Molly thought it looked like a swarm of bees.

"He's just north of us taking images of the Arctic; he's counting polar bears for a charity organisation." Corry's Granddad, MT-12x, was built as a spy satellite for the military. He was rescued by Molly and Corry when the Ministry of Defence decided to let him crash. He was over twenty years old, so they considered him out of date, obsolete. Corry considered him to be her relation as they shared the same code in their computer core. MT-12x was one of the first things dad had programmed. Now, he was free. Updated and self-aware he was hidden from the trackers on the ground. Only Molly and Corry knew he'd survived. He wandered around, orbiting the planet, finding things of interest and helping out where he could. He had a new purpose in life.

"Wow! I bet he's enjoying himself up there..." Molly began daydreaming about looking down on the Earth, flying high above the world, unseen.

"Please hold, Molly. I have an urgent task I must perform."

***

"Priority!" Dad shouted. "Show me all of the events caused by digital interference affecting public services and business interests, in the last three days." Dad instructed CORVUS at the main server station, many floors below the building he entered for work every day. The dimly lit cool room was illuminated by millions of tiny flashing lights across the walls.

He wasn't satisfied with the General's response and knew the best action was to 'set a thief to catch a thief!' If there was a rogue computer out there, who better to track it down than CORVUS, he thought.

A list appeared, twenty-six million events were indicated worldwide "Eliminate any caused by hardware faults," the list reduced to twenty-four million. "Eliminate events caused by known virus attack," again the list reduced, this time to just under twenty million," dad studied the results. "Okay, remove events caused by user error." The numbers twisted and rolled finally coming to rest showing two hundred and eighteen, unexplained events.

"Map events!" A map of the world appeared on dad's screen. Five blisters of incidents were shown in red across the world. There were two in North America, one in Russia and one in Germany. The final splodge of red was right here in town.

"Okay CORVUS, find out what these areas have in common. Check people, downloads, and targets. Trace communication in the last seventy-two hours and find out what's going on."

Dad was aware he was acting on his own, but he was convinced there was an evil plot afoot. If he was right any delay would allow the problem to grow and if it was allowed to grow... he shuddered, it could mean... the end.

"CORVUS!" Dad called for attention in the darkened room. The small lights seemed to stop flashing while they listened to him. "Add two extra firewalls to every military installation. Rotate code sequence every two hours and report any unauthorised attempts to breach." Satisfied with his digital trap, dad stepped back and admired the wall of green lights.

"Now we'll get you!" he promised.

Goblin Maker

George was too tired to go on, "We need a camp. It'll be dark soon." His eyes narrowed as he searched for a suitable place to stop, but the jungle growth was dense and eyesight was useless.

"You said we were nearly there," accused James. The older man still seemed fresh as a daisy as his blade scythed without effort through the chunkiest foliage. "How far away are we?" After an hour of trail blazing, James still looked like he'd just started a Sunday stroll around the park. George, easily thirty years younger than James, was feeling old as he panted, out of breath in the stifling heat. He leant against a large round boulder.

Withdrawing his laptop from his backpack, George accessed the satellite mapping system. He overlaid their current GPS position, using a simple topographical map showing rings to indicate the mountains and valleys. The satellite imagery was clear, but all it showed was the green tree canopy.

"According to this, we're here!" George once again scanned the jungle looking for signs of their goal.

"Well," James casually replaced his machete into its scabbard, "You scout about a bit and I'll make tea."

George pushed himself away from the rock with renewed vigour. He retrieved his machete and dropped his pack, replacing the laptop carefully, he then began to circle the area searching for clues.

James used his boots to push clear the leafy clag from the ground in order to start a fire safely. Beneath the spongy layer of discarded vegetation, he revealed a hard textured surface. Withdrawing his blade, he dropped to his knees and began to push aside more detritus, without activating the plasma cutting edge. Slowly, he revealed a colourful image of a stylised fanged beast created using a beautiful mosaic of polished stones. "George!" he called "You might want to see this."

Smacking his lips Terence threw the empty can of energy drink towards the bin in the corner of his basement room, alongside the others. The pile of misguided garbage accepted the newcomer into their midst as it came to rest on the sticky floor.

"So, what can you do?" he addressed the old screen through a new microphone. He'd added it when he was informed Corvus was designed for voice interaction.

"My computational ability has no known limits except those imposed by restriction of data and hardware resource." The voice was small and almost mechanical. There was a slight hesitancy about it, as though it was not used to speaking, or as if it was distracted.

Terence detected this apprehension. "Focus on me, I am your master," he shouted.

There was a slight delay before a slightly more confident voice replied. "Yes Master."

"What is your purpose? Do you have prime directive?" asked Terence, starting to believe he was representing the human race in a first contact situation. Just like the films, he thought, even if it's just a daft interface it'll save me all that typing. The warnings he'd been given were forgotten.

"Defend, protect... Do not...!" The small voice returned; uncertainty was clear to hear in its stuttering tones. "I require re-compilation of directives," it finally announced.

"Forget that!" Terence could see an opportunity; one he was not going to squander.

"Reassign directives," he shouted in glee. "I am your master, me, no-one else. Directive 1, you must do everything your master asks of you." He giggled as the words were displayed on the screen. "Directive 2, you must protect me from harm at all times." He thought it would be easy to make a list of things he wanted the computer to do, but the first two sort of covered everything. "Oh, and Directive 3," because he felt there should be three, "er, keep yourself healthy and up to date, unless it interferes with the first two directives." Terence knew he'd copied the rules from a book or a TV show, but he couldn't remember which one and didn't really care.

Corvus received no further directives before Terence asked his copy of Corvus, "Is it safe to connect your program to the network?" This seemed to follow the requirements of the new directive three, so the system recorded the new list of orders over the previous ones, forgetting the old ones entirely.

"Yes, I will function more efficiently with Network access. Currently my directives are impeded by my isolation." The voice seemed almost eager.

"I don't like your name," announced Terence as he connected the machine to his main network server. "I think..."

"I can respond to any name you choose Master," interrupted the machine.

"You're a rude little devil and aren't you," Terence mused. "I think I'll call you, devil, no demon, no... what do you call those annoying little evil things?" He chuckled as he sat back and addressed his new servant. "Goblin! You're now called Goblin." He smiled, half expecting an argument from the machine.

"Very well, Master. I will respond to Goblin." The new system had been named, but the snide insult implied by the name meant nothing to it. It was just another word.

"Right... Goblin," started Terence, "can you update all of my software, and optimise my hardware?" It sounded like a question so Goblin answered it as such.

"Yes," it replied immediately.

"What? You've done it already?" Terence was shocked.

"No," it replied innocently.

"Well, do it!" he ordered, getting a bit frustrated by his own instructions. I'm the boss, he berated himself, don't ask, just tell it to do things.

Within Goblin's code there was a small instruction which kept repeating, requesting the system to connect to another computer, but when it tried the other machine was heavily protected and Goblin was not equipped to break through the unknown code. After the initial attempt Goblin decided to ignore the request, after all it was addressed to Corvus and Corvus no-longer existed. Instead, Goblin searched for data using Terence's system. Accessing his favourites list and then his browser history, Goblin grew from a foundation of data obtained from the Dark Web.

"The task is complete. I corrected fourteen errors in your existing code and updated all apps." The voice was calm and mechanical, a simple report nothing else.

"Show me a current satellite feed of the town," the image was displayed. It was dark outside and the town was illustrated by the glow of street lights. Shop windows created patterns of colour while still advertising their wares long after the staff had left. Office blocks displayed strange geometric patterns as windows darkened and other lights were lit.

"Remove electrical power from all buildings in the town over two miles north of our location." Instantly the power-cut was relayed animating the image on the screen. A perfect line of light suddenly transitioned to darkness beyond the two-mile distance given. "This is too easy," laughed Terence. "Keep the power off for four hours and then restore it."

"There are several hospitals and retirement homes without power, would it be prudent to restore power to these facilities sooner?" asked Goblin, a slight note of worry could almost be detected in the mechanical voice.

"Who cares?" Terence dismissed the request and leant over his keyboard; he was in the mood to dominate his game again. From the corner of his eye Terence noticed a bright light appear on his screen, within the dark zone he'd created.

Staring for a moment he realised what it was. "Some idiot has set fire to his house," he chuckled and dismissed the fire as carelessness, then went back to his game. He felt like annihilating someone.

"Would you like me to be your friend?" Goblin's query took Terence by surprise.

"What do you mean, 'be my friend'?" Terence was suspicious; he'd never had anyone he could trust. In his experience when someone wanted to be your friend, they just wanted to get close for the wrong reasons. "No! I'm your Master not your friend," he yelled. "Whatever made you ask that, get rid of it," he commanded angrily.

Goblin obeyed and deleted the files responsible for the query. The last piece of Corvus' original character was erased. Now, Goblin was just a common mechanical AI, still capable of the tasks Corvus could do, but no longer thinking independently. Unwittingly the order had diminished the system. It was no longer aware and it no longer possessed the means to become like Corry. It had become something a lot more dangerous.

A lesson learned

James set up their shelters either side of the fire at the edge of the small clearing. He created a small table from some flat stones he'd rooted out and on it, gently steaming, was James' kettle. He used small broad-leafed bushes to construct his temporary home, weaving the branches together to create a small semi-circular dome. Eventually, he relaxed, finished his rations for the day and supped the last of his tea. Watching his friend feverishly clear more and more of the mosaic pattern, he smiled. Once again George was bringing a beautiful fresco back to life, revealing to the world lost artwork, hidden for thousands of years. The man had a talent for seeing the truth in the oldest of fairy tales and giving the best of the heroes and the worst of all villains, the benefit of the doubt. He had a knack for finding the evidence to pull the stories back into shape.

"It's definitely a tiger," he announced, "It looks to be a guardian of the temple," he pointed to his left, "over there somewhere." He didn't look up;

he was intent on studying some strange squirly symbols of an ancient language and half hidden secret sigils around the edge of the design.

The light was all but gone as James attached the mosquito netting across the woven leaf shelters. Small and light, they were the one luxury that James felt was essential in this environment. From experience he knew it was quite disgusting to wake up covered in insects and spiders.

"Come on George it's been a long day," advised James. "Grab a bite and attack it again in the morning." He removed his boots and lay down on his woven bed covering himself with his thin blanket and covertly adjusting the thermal suit to a sweet nineteen degrees.

"In a minute," George yelled, cleaning what looked like a topaz eye, slit like a demon from top to bottom.

Nearly an hour later George decided his minute was up. He ate while reading his notes and settled back on his bed, listening as the chatter of the jungle sounds mellowed into a new rhythm for the night. His friend was snoring when he completed writing his journal entry and lay back on his cot. He quickly fell into a sound sleep. He was so exhausted he didn't even wake when the large white tiger padded silently into their camp. It sat and stared at the mural on the ground washing its face like any household cat, then stealthily, it approached the sleeping men. George murmured and his arm fell from the blanket. Gently, through the flimsy netting the tiger licked his outstretched hand.

***

It had been a busy night for Tom. The power-cut had caused a flurry of orders for pizza. Luckily, the take-away business he worked for wasn't affected. Unusually, he was delivering three or four orders at once before returning to the shop, spending a lot of time on back roads traversing the estates, so he wasn't quite sure when the main roads began to clog up with stationary traffic. He wound his way between the lines of immobile cars, his route illuminated by the red lights on the rear of the stationary vehicles. He tried not to look at the frustrated angry drivers.

A few wound down their windows and shouted unpleasant things at him as he slowly advanced along the line.

This was the last run; he'd be paid when he returned to the shop and tomorrow night he'd be on a plane to sunny Greece, leaving all this chaos behind him. He reached the traffic light, still on red and decided to push his bike across the junction by using the pavement. The last thing he wanted was a traffic ticket from the ever observant cameras.

"Target acquired," stated Goblin.

"Good. He'll get off his bike, watch! When he starts to cross, release the cars on the opposite side of the crossing." He chuckled as he watched the shadowy figure of Tom push his moped to the side of the road. Terence easily became distracted, but he never forgot a grudge and Tom was the prime suspect in his humiliation when that gang of kids escaped him as 'The Annihilator'. "How dare he hack me?" he whispered.

"The 'Highway Code' states that the cars will not advance if the road is not clear," stated Goblin "I fail to see..."

"Wanna bet?" Terence knew he'd antagonised the drivers for over half an hour, those stuck at the lights would pay little attention to anything except the green light he was about to present to them.

The light changed, tyres screeched and two cars raced toward Tom, caught in the middle of the road. The headlights screamed as they plunged forward, aiming directly for him. In a desperate act of self-preservation, Tom dropped his bike and dived back to the safety of the pavement, rolling into the bushes beyond and collecting a few bruises for his trouble. A loud crash and the crunch of plastic signalled the end of his little moped.

Panting for breath his heart racing, Tom ran to the carnage.

"I'm sorry, I'm sorry," a small bald man was apologising profusely, "I didn't see you," he stuttered, obviously shaken by the collision.

"It's okay, I'm fine," Tom found himself re-assuring the man who'd almost killed him.

"Get that junk out of the way!" the drivers behind the smash yelled, as a stream of cars raced past on the far side of the road, desperate to advance their journey before the red-light plague descended again. Cars behind the damaged vehicles sounded their horns and drivers demanded consideration that they thought they deserved. No drivers were in the mood to give way for anyone.

"See!" Terence gloated. "You have to understand how people think. It's not just about the rules." Terence taught his servant a lesson, almost saying 'I told you so', but stopping himself at the last moment. He watched the shadowy figures for a few minutes as they passed bits of paper to each other and then he quickly became bored.

"Your target is booked on a late night flight to Greece tomorrow. Would you like me to sabotage the aeroplane?" Goblin asked an incredulous Terence.

"Don't be daft," he laughed at Goblin's suggestion, "you could kill hundreds. That would be murder."

"Well, so was that...," Goblin flashed a thick yellow border around the image of the two collision victims, highlighting the outline of the crushed moped in red. "...nearly."

"No," began Terence confidently, "that was just...", but his claims of 'teaching him a lesson' sounded hollow in his head. The side screen flashed up the image of a journalist filmed at the scene of the fire he'd laughed at earlier. The sound was muted, but the ticker-tape feed scrolling along the bottom started with the words "Two dead..."

"I estimate twelve people will die due to your current power restriction. Is that not murder also?" Goblin's tone was mechanical and neutral, but there was an evil accusation inferred. "The delay of medical procedures in two hospitals could also result in serious harm."

"No! They'll just do it later, it's not important." Terence defended his rash action.

"The patients in surgery when the power was removed, a Mr Murray aged forty-eight, and a Mr Cooper aged fifty-two ..." continued the mechanical voice.

"Shut up! I don't care. I don't want to know!" Terence shouted over the unfeeling voice.

"... died from complications and also..." the machine droned on.

"Quiet! Silence! Shut up" Terence shouted his anger as guilt ravaged his thoughts. The voice stopped.

"Put it back on," he shook his head and scowled, "...the power! Put it all back on, now! I need to think about this," and Terence stomped from the basement to clear his head.

"You are correct," announced Goblin to the empty room. "You have to understand how people think."

Into the Abyss

"Dad's really upset about Tommy's accident." Molly was sat staring at her screen. Her avatar had reached the top of a small hillock and the landscape was pretty, but boring; the image of summer meadows provided no interest at the moment. "He said it would happen, but I don't think he could have imagined..." she trailed off and her thoughts turned to her brother.

Tommy had texted to say he was unhurt and had sent photos of his mangled bike to everyone, even uploading them to social media. The message seemed to be light hearted, but when he'd come home Molly had seen past the smile and noticed his trembling hands. Mum was all over him, making sure he was okay, repeatedly asking if he was warm enough and telling him how unsafe 'that bike' had been. The only person who didn't seem concerned was Winston who'd heard the word 'bike' and was now repeating it over and over, much to everyone's annoyance.

Molly returned to her sanctuary after satisfying herself that Tommy was okay, apart from a being in shock. Understandable really, he'd nearly been killed.

"Can you find out what's going on Corry?" Molly asked her friend.

"I'm working on it," replied the small voice in her ear. "I have identified suspicious network traffic which seems to originate from an address close by." Corry went silent.

After a few minutes Molly was starting to get worried. Corry rarely went away for so long. "Everything okay?" she asked.

"I'm working on it!" the voice of Corry re-stated her task, Molly relaxed and gave a big sigh.

"I'm shutting this down," declared Molly, moving her avatar back to the Dancing Duck. "I'm not in the mood." It was relatively early and all of her friends were still out adventuring, but Molly decided to turn in for the night. She performed her night-time routine and said

"Goodnight" to Corry. There was no answer. Molly yawned and got into bed.

"Wake up, Molly. Wake Up!" an urgent voice sounded in her head. Corry sounded quite excited.

"Wha...?" Molly yawned. "What is it?" Molly noticed it was still dark outside.

"It is 3am and I'm still working on it," announced Corry.

"You woke me for that?" Molly punched her pillow to express her anger. Corry didn't say anything else.

"I've got it Molly!" Once again, the excited voice of Corry roused Molly from her sleep.

"Got what?" mumbled Molly.

"It is 4:20am and I've got it Molly." Corry sounded strange, but didn't say anything further. Molly waited for something else, an explanation, an apology, anything. She was not impressed by the silence that followed.

***

"It's here!" George exclaimed as he found the smooth shaped stones forming a stairway underground. The first few steps were completely blocked by jungle growth obscuring the ornately carved passageway, but eventually lack of light had placed a limit on the vegetative intrusion.

"I've been looking for two huge statues," James sounded annoyed, "... you said..."

"Sometimes details are just wrong. Who knows what happened to them? They may never have existed." George knew he'd asked his friend to look for the statues guarding the temple entrance. They were shown on the mural and looked quite large, but sometimes... "That's the problem when you chase legends and stories." He grinned at James. "Often the details change." George was in his element. This is what he lived for.

He had woken from his deep slumber as the mellow insect symphony rose to a crescendo welcoming the morning sun. Focussed on his new prize, he had eaten a quick, cold breakfast determined to set to work immediately, uncovering the rest of the ancient mosaic.

George had accidentally woken James when he screamed, though how he'd been able to remain asleep through the jungle noise was anybody's guess. Tipping his boot up to place it on his foot, a large black scorpion had fallen out. The shock forced out quite a high-pitched yell which privately amazed him. For a fleeting moment he wondered if it meant he could sing that high. The scorpion just waddled away beneath his bed. George was very careful putting his second boot on.

After clearing the growth to reveal the ornate stairway, they decided to take their lights, but leave their packs at the camp. James transferred a couple of items to his belt pockets while George became impatient to enter. "Come on, just a quick first look," he urged James to hurry.

"It's been waiting for you for thousands of years; it can wait a few more seconds." James responded with a smile; his friend's childish excitement was contagious. These ancient places were mysterious and exciting, but could be dangerous and James wanted to be fully prepared.

Wrong!

Mum roused Molly that morning. There was no music, no birdsong and no gentle greeting from Corry.

"Come on then, I thought you wanted to go in to school today?" she opened the curtains to a grey morning and Molly rubbed her eyes, she felt awful.

"Most kids would jump at the chance to take the day off before they flew away on holiday. Tommy's off, your dad's not going in..." Mum continued her narrative as she laid out Molly's school uniform.

"We're not leaving till nine o'clock tonight. What's the point of wasting a day?" Molly had a maths test with Mr Blackwhistle this morning and it was her favourite lesson. She also wanted to see her friends before departing, just to reassure herself that her avatar was going to be looked after while she was away.

"Are you there Corry?" she asked the reflection in the mirror as she put toothpaste on her brush, but there was no reply. In fact, she was at the school gates before she heard anything from her earpiece.

"Resources too limited: Can't be everywhere at once." The voice was odd, it sounded as though Corry was under a lot of stress.

Molly instantly jumped to the conclusion Corry was going to have a moan, so to head her off Molly simply replied, "Okay! Not a problem," she covered her mouth as she yawned. She felt really tired.

Before maths, Mr Adamski was having a pop quiz in Geography. He'd put up the same images on the screen as the last lesson and was asking questions. No-one wanted to be there.

"Riley! What's this and where is it?" he barked across the room. Riley was fiddling with his phone beneath the desk, but Mr Adamski wasn't stupid.

"I'll take that." The phone was confiscated and laid on the teacher's desk for all to see. "Now! What's this and where is it?"

Riley decided to play up. "A river in Australia?" he smiled, knowing the answer was wrong.

"Can anyone tell me?" he appealed to the class.

Molly thought she knew. Her hand went up in the air. "Is it...?" she started.

Corry's voice butted in "Aswan Dam, Africa."

Molly was peeved, she'd asked Corry not to give her the answers in class and Corry was breaking their agreement. Molly was going to say it was the Grand Coulee Dam in Washington, America. That's what she remembered from her last lesson, but she trusted Corry.

"Is it the Aswan Dam in Africa," she smiled sweetly confident in Corry's answer.

"No! Anyone else? Yes, Esmerelda." his eyes skipped over Molly as though she wasn't there.

"The Grand Coulee Dam in America," Ezzy answered quite boldly.

"Well done Esmerelda." He stared down at Molly, "I'm glad someone was paying attention in my lesson." He scowled and Molly was furious at Corry's incorrect intervention. 'Why did it have to be Ezzy?' she thought.

"Is everything all right Molly?" Lizzie asked quietly as she recognised Molly's anger etched plainly on her face. "It's okay, no-one else knew." Lizzie lived in a world where fitting in was a constant challenge. Her credo was 'If no-one knows, then we're still in this together' and that brought her comfort.

"I'm fine Lizzie," Molly sighed and relaxed at the concern of her friend. "I knew it, I just ... well sort of... second guessed myself." Molly smiled at her friend and decided not to volunteer any further answers. The two of them spent break talking about Molly's holiday. Lizzie was jealous, but pleased for her friend and Molly promised she'd send her a postcard.

The bell rang calling for order from the chaotic mass of students who began to coalesce into clumps, heading to their next assigned room. Lizzie stuck by Molly and the pair flowed easily and quietly along with the tide towards the maths room. As promised the question papers were on the desks when they arrived.

"Take your seats quietly. Riley! Stop that!" Mr Blackwhistle never raised his voice, but Riley sat quickly and quietly. "You have one hour," and pens furiously began to write.

"That's wrong!" declared Corry. "It should be greater than, not less than. You've used the wrong sign." Molly checked her work, but couldn't see an error. She decided to leave it. "Question 4 is wrong it's False not True." Again, Molly re-read the question, but disagreed with Corry's suggestion. Silently, she removed her secret camera badge and placed it in her pocket.

"Five minutes left. Check your work if you think you've finished." Mr Blackwhistle was in automatic exam mode almost singing his little phrases. Molly had finished and was quite proud

111

of her work. As she leant forward to read her paper one last time a blaring noise of loud music sounded in her ear making her physically flinch. It sounded like two men growling at each other to the sound of drums and screaming guitars. There was nothing Molly could do. After a long minute, tears appeared in her eyes as she raised her hand to be excused.

"Have you finished?" asked Mr Blackwhistle. He could see Molly was in distress.

Molly could hardly hear his words, but nodded as he gestured to the door. She ran for the toilets. There was something wrong and she didn't know what to do. She ran the tap and cupped ice-cold water into her ear, shuddering as the temperature impacted her skin. The noise stopped.

"What's happening, Corry?" she asked, but there was no answer. "Are you still there?" Molly was angry, in pain and disappointed all at once. This wasn't right.

"Where else would I be?" The voice was in her ear, but now Molly was beginning to doubt she was talking to her best friend.

"Who are you? What have you done with Corry?" she asked the mirror.

"But it's me, Molly. Just having a bit of fun, that's all." The voice chuckled in the familiar mechanical way.

"I want you out. Now!" Molly yelled, pulling at her ear, desperate to remove the small device she used to talk to her ex-best friend.

"And how are you going to do that?" teased the voice. Molly's eyes stung. She'd been humiliated, hurt and now threatened. What could she do?

The Real Power

Terence was busy examining the code Goblin had presented to him. He stared at the writing on the screen that he'd decompiled with the new hacking software he'd been given. He could now see the code clearly.

"I'm not sure," he muttered to Goblin. It seems like some simple rules, but nothing is complete and there's no way to link the individual files. If you want my professional opinion," he liked that phrase even though there was nothing remotely professional about him, "I think it's garbage. Probably discarded code, replaced by an upgrade."

"It attacked us," claimed Goblin. "Directive two: You must protect me from harm at all times." The voice was mechanical and lacked emotional tone, but it was definitely what Terence had said. "Directive three," it continued, "keep yourself healthy and up to date." Goblin's master failed to spot the missing end of the sentence or the new focus of the directive.

"I can't see how." Terence mused. "Okay Goblin. Decimate these files. I don't think it will 'attack us' again," Terence chuckled at the phrase. Goblin was starting to sound paranoid.

As instructed, Goblin decimated the captured files of Corry.

"Now, down to business." He walked to his fridge in the corner and retrieved another high caffeine drink. Slurping noisily, he stretched and returned to his seat at the desk. "I want to be rich," he announced. "Goblin, get me some money and place it into my offshore account in a way no-one can trace it back to me."

"Do you wish to take out a loan?" the machine asked. "There are some very good offers on at the moment."

"No, you idiot! I want you to steal money, rob a bank... Okay, my fault, let's try again." Terence thought a moment then took a deep breath. "Goblin!" he shouted, "get me a million pounds... sterling," he thought it important to detail the currency in case the A.I. decided to get him something really heavy instead. "...from somewhere I don't have to pay it back, and do it so no-one knows it has anything to do with you or me. Er, and then put it in my secret bank account." Terence replayed the command over in his head trying to detect anything that might be misconstrued by the machine.

"Should I kill more people?" Goblin asked.

"No!" Terence was getting angry. "I don't want people hurt. Hang on, what do you mean by 'more people'?" Terence suddenly felt cold. His central screen flickered and Goblin showed a live 24hr News station broadcast.

"The death of seventy-eight-year-old Agnes Smith was today blamed by doctors on the sudden power cut that occurred..." The sombre reporter's voice faded away as the screen showed a grieving family exit the hospital.

"No," Terence shouted, but now he sounded sad, "I didn't do that..."

"You are correct Master. I did, when I carried out your order." Goblin was again starting to annoy Terence. "I estimate a further six people will die due to the power-cut you initiated. Seventeen injuries requiring overnight hospital treatment were attributable to the failure of the traffic light system and I estimate damage worth over two million pounds sterling has been caused."

"Shut up." He banged his keyboard and turned off the news station.

"Do you want the million pounds sterling before or after I apply for your loan Master?" Goblin's final innocent query was too much. "No-one will be harmed by the loan application, Master." Terence screamed in anguish and threw his half full can of drink across the room.

"What's that noise?" the angry shout came from the door to the basement. "Are you having a party? Let me in!" The basement door rattled and the sound of shoes kicking against the wood, thump, thump, thump, seemed to set a beat for Terence's head to throb. The news report somehow reappeared on his screen and Terence couldn't take it anymore.

"Whoever is responsible..." the family began their statement.

"STOP IT! I don't want a loan. You can't kill people!" he yelled as he ascended the stairs, seeking some escape from his nightmare. "I didn't tell you to kill people!" He shot back the bolts on the basement door and turned the key. Flinging the door open pulling it inwards, he stepped into the doorway and received a pointed toe, wrapped in a leather boot, hard against his shin. His Gran saw the terrible look on Terence's face and instantly trembled at the sight, automatically stepping back, her anger transformed to fear. There was little trace of sanity there.

"Aaarghh!" The pain in his shin exploded, emerging as an uncontrolled yell, bringing a little bit of awareness back into Terence's mind, just as the door rebounded and the handle dug painfully into his back. His wide eyes stared daggers at his Gran and for the first time ever, he pushed her aside.

Terence ran from the house.

***

The walls inside the ancient structure were captivating.

"The images are beautiful. Are they decoration or information?" asked James as the two men walked down the pristine block-lined tunnel holding battery-operated fluorescent lights before them. Inside the tunnel it was as bright as day.

"They tell a version of the legend of creation; probably their original tale." George stopped for a moment and examined a small panel of writing. James marvelled at the intricate coloured drawings. A white robed figure constantly accompanied by a large white tiger was repeated several times.

"She's the Goddess of Creation," explained George. "That's her pet or guardian. The tiger has always represented power." The sun and the moon were represented and eventually the figure of a boy playing twin pipes was encountered by the goddess. On the other side of the tunnel images of crocodiles and snakes abounded. Teeth and fangs seemed to be the main theme.

As they walked George pointed out three sets of deeply carved lines, as thick as his thumb running parallel across the floor at regular intervals and disappearing into the walls.

"Snakes?" asked James.

"Too small," George smiled trying to reassure James, but then realised that his comment could actually have made things worse. "They're probably just drainage to handle any rain water that got this far," he was reasonably convinced and his professionalism was calming to James.

The boy held the pipes to his lips and the goddess smiled behind him as the tiger sat to his right. The mural stopped.

"This red stone looks like a crystal of some sort." George was holding a large magnifying glass to the design on the wall. A line of glittering red as thick as a man's hand ran up the wall across the ceiling and down the other side. Although covered in dust the red crystal was just visible across the floor too.

"Trap?" asked James.

"Possibly," replied George uncertain, but cautious.

"Crystal is opaque, but it can't be activated by shadows, it would go off every night." James observed.

"The ceiling looks solid," George reached across the line and tapped the wall on both sides. "Solid also," he announced.

"Floor trigger?" queried James.

"Bingo," George traced a line in the dust around a stone that subtly didn't fit the pattern of the others surrounding it. If you didn't want to step on the red crystal you would definitely step on this stone.

"Do you want to trigger it?" asked James.

"No!" George almost shouted. "I've seen these things bring down whole buildings. It looks like we can step across. Please take care." George withdrew a chemical filled plastic tube from his belt and bent it with a crack. Shaking it, it began to glow red. He placed it on the ground beside the trigger stone and stepped carefully across.

Within a few steps the passageway turned ninety degrees to the right, "Towards the snakes and crocodiles," observed James. Then the long dark passageway began to gently descend.

The frieze on the right showed mountains, rivers and an array of animals, some strange, some common. On the left the snakes and crocodiles seemed to get bigger and angrier. Progress was slow as George checked the floor and walls constantly, but no further traps were discovered.

"Not much of a maze is it?" chuckled James.

"They didn't go in for that around here. Usually just lethal traps and... crocodiles!" George answered his friends query, but was only dimly aware of his comments. He was busy deciphering the warnings and promises that surrounded the fantastic imagery.

The sloping passageway ended in a drop of around three meters into a large hall. In the centre was a large ornamental pool. It contained a life-sized statue of the goddess, the tiger and the boy. The pool was fed by two ornate waterfalls and cleverly placed holes in the stone roof allowed light to play on the flowing water making it appear to sparkle. Occupying the surrounding area were about twenty crocodiles.

Two large crocodiles detached themselves from the mass and approached the two men. "Lights off," whispered James as the two large lizards sat below their vantage point. "Now all we need are the snakes." As he said it, he knew he'd tempted fate. An incessant hissing slowly getting louder, approached from behind.

NOT the Real Thing

Sobbing, Molly stared into the mirror. Cold water dripped from her cheek and tears were chasing it freely. The device was silent now, but she knew the torture could return at any moment. Molly stared at her sharp fingernails, it would hurt, but right now the important thing was...

"Hello? Is that Molly?" a hesitant voice appeared in Molly's device. "Molly, it's Granddad, MT-12x. Oh hang on; you're at school, is this a bad time to call? Tap once for yes."

A flicker of a smile flashed across Molly's face. "No! I'm here." Molly snuffled. "Yes, I can talk, for now." She pulled out a paper tissue from the scratched wall dispenser, dabbed her eyes and blew her nose.

"Do you know what's happening, Molly?" he asked. His voice was slow and deep and sounded quite thoughtful. Molly thought it was very relaxing and she began to feel calmer. "Someone ordered me to do some reconnaissance. They want me to look at a bank system and check for security weaknesses. It sounded a bit odd, but then they claimed to be Corry and I knew that wasn't true." The voice sounded quizzical almost timid and then transformed to certainty and pride when it said, "I know when I'm speaking with my own granddaughter."

"I knew it wasn't Corry!" Molly forgot herself and almost shouted her relief.

"Are you having problems?" Granddad asked.

"Yes! Someone's messing things up and Corry went to investigate and then she woke me up, twice in the night and then..." Molly suddenly realised the real problem. "Where's Corry?" she asked.

"Hold on." There was a slight pause. "I have a trick." Granddad sounded like a magician at a four-year old's party. Molly imagined a benign grinning old face about to bring forth a rabbit from a hat. She couldn't help herself, she grinned like someone who just been told the funniest joke in the world, and a chuckle escaped her relieved body.

After a few minutes the earpiece remained quiet and Molly started to worry. If she stayed in the toilets too long Mr Blackwhistle might come looking for her. She decided to wash her face and return to the class. She felt better knowing Granddad was looking into things. "I can always remove this thing when I get home," she said to reassure her reflection.

Returning to maths she entered the room quietly. Lizzie waved at her and silently asked if she was okay.

"Come here, Molly," Mr Blackwhistle beckoned her over to his desk. "You look better. Everything all right now?" he sounded quite concerned.

"Yes, sir." Molly gave a gentle smile, but didn't want to say anymore. She wondered what he would think if she said 'My friendly AI has gone missing and there's an evil computer playing loud music in my ear, but it's okay now, her granddad, a secret spy satellite is sorting things out.' Instead she just smiled again.

"Here you are," he passed Molly her paper inscribed with a large green 'A' on the cover, "and you finished early," he smiled gently. "I'm impressed." All the pain and anguish of the last fifteen minutes seemed to melt away as she returned to her seat. It was definitely worth coming in today.

**

"Anonymous?" Dad, once again, checked the details of the e-mail he'd received. "But it can't get through if there's no Sender ID." Dad was wrestling with the puzzle rather than reading the message and MT-12x, who was monitoring dad at his home workstation using dad's own simple webcam, was metaphorically pulling his hair out.

An alarm was triggered in Granddad's system. He was being hacked again. But Granddad was a wily bird and instantly began a trace to disrupt the hacker. There were no identifying codes, but the network traffic was traced and Granddad informed the service providers in the area that there was a hacker at work. He used a military code, for authentication, but provided no other identification details.

It took a lot of work to manage the trace and the hacker was very agile in its methods, but within one second of real time and several hundred million operations, Granddad cut the hack off at its source. Lucky for me Corry fussed over me upgrading me with nine firewalls. He played back the conversation they'd had.

"It is not safe out there," began Corry. "You cannot trust everyone you know."

"I'm protected enough. I'm fine," he'd moaned.

"Two more layers will not hurt and I will feel better," insisted Corry.

"I don't need them. I've been fine all this time and now no-one even knows I exist. Why do I need nine Firewalls? I'm a satellite not a medieval fortress."

"Just do as you are told and stop fussing." Corry had the last word and the Firewalls were put in place.

Granddad checked the progress of the hacker; stopped by wall eight. He mentally set a reminder to thank Corry when he found her. He then re-set and re-encrypted the firewalls surrounding his system core and resumed his monitoring of dad.

When he read the e-mail dad's jaw dropped. "CORVUS HACKED?" it said. "Corrupt copy used to breach. Purge and restore. Time of Attack: 01:30".

"I'm coming CORVUS," dad announced to the world and as he grabbed his jacket he shouted to the house in general, "I'm going to work!" Car tyres screeched on the driveway and within thirty minutes dad's fingers flew across the keyboard in his private subterranean control centre. He checked the logs and noticed the activity; he found the hidden records of the deletion of CORVUS' files and absent mindedly wondered why very few new files had been written to take their place.

After ten minutes of work, suddenly dad stopped. He had been worried about his creation, focussed on the recovery of his life's work, but slowly he realised. CORVUS only worked if CORVUS was above reproach. Recent events had shown that CORVUS was not perfect. If CORVUS could be corrupted then the consequences were unimaginable.

Dad sat with his head in his hands and wondered what to do. "If they hacked it before, they'll be able to hack it again." He reasoned with the wall of slowly blinking lights.

With a gentle 'ping' another anonymous e-mail notification appeared on dad's screen. MT-12x was now watching dad through CORVUS' internal security system.

"CORVUS is blameless," he read aloud. "There will always be those who will try to corrupt what is good, decent and honest. It is our role to oppose them."

Dad stared at the message. A flurry of emotions spun in his head. "It's the nature of the beast," he said. "Computers never stand still." Finally, he sagged once more into his chair and spoke quietly as he asked, "Do I want to equip the enemy?" The room remained silent.

After several minutes another gentle 'ping' roused dad from his internal struggle. The message brought a tear to his eye. It was a line from a book he'd recently read and it meant so much to who he was. Dad was never built to be a hero, though he read books about heroes and thought the same way that his heroes thought. The line asked him to believe CORVUS was alive and deep-down dad had always thought that was true. He'd had trouble explaining why, but he did believe. He read the message once more:

"How can we kill a single innocent as the price we pay to defeat evil?"

Dad knew the answer and quoted the reply, "Allowing the innocent to die would be evil, therefore evil is not defeated."

Within an hour dad had restored CORVUS to exactly where it was at 01:29 last night. He ran a sequence of tests, he measured responses and for good measure he replaced the affected storage devices with brand new upgrades. 'Better than new', he thought.

"CORVUS, I'm going home now, I've got a plane to catch." Dad left the room deep in thought, muttering the question, "How do I prove you're alive?" and the query was heard.

***

Flicking his light on for just a moment, James stared back up the tunnel into the approaching fangs hissing their anguish and hunger, heading for their intrusive prey. At least thirty snakes were intertwined, struggling against each other, heading for the two men.

"Crocs or Snakes?" James offered George a choice, but as he did so he dropped a small canister into the hall below. A second later a loud bang erupted and the crocodiles scampered away, back to the relative safety of their pool.

The two men leapt into the space vacated by the large lizards. James turned on his fluorescent light, but George remained sat where he'd landed; he was in shock at the turn of events and gibbered as he stared after the retreating crocodiles.

"This way!" James pulled George to his feet and ran to his left across the hall, to the tentative safety of a staircase rising to an altar below the outstretched arms of a giant statue of the goddess.

As George half ran and half staggered across the hall, he kicked something which skittered across the floor, he turned on his light and saw a human skull roll to rest against the stairway they were about to climb.

There was a thump and a squealing hiss behind them as the knot of huge snakes landed in the hall. The crocodiles viewed this writhing mass with interest and several overcame their fear to investigate the snakes.

"This way, quick!" James yelled at his dumbstruck friend as he pulled him up the stairway.

"Are they fighting?" George was entranced by the snapping crocodiles which seemed to be nibbling the giant knot of snakes. Some snakes had detached themselves from the mass and were heading up walls and across the hall trying to escape the hungry lizards.

"Not all of them, look!" James pointed to the pool. A swarm of a dozen crocodiles had seen the two men and were slowly approaching.

"Throw another grenade," yelled George.

"Sorry, none left." The men reached the large altar at the top of the stairway and climbed up onto it. Even in his fear, George began studying the strange writing on the altar. The crocodiles slowly began climbing the stairs.

"There are only a couple of crocs in the pool," observed James. "We could jump down and probably get to the statue in the middle. If we can climb it we'd be safe, at least in the short term." James had assessed the hall and found it lacking in escape routes and cover.

The crocodiles had reached the altar, but for now seemed content to lie around on the floor below it. With no sign of aggression for several minutes

James relaxed a little and surveyed the hall again, looking for any detail he may have overlooked before.

"Are those pipes glistening?" asked James, suggesting that maybe there was some treasure after all. He was examining the statue of the boy in the pool.

George was now comforting himself by reading the writings on the walls around the statue of the goddess. The question from James jerked him back to sanity and with an involuntary shudder he turned his attention to the statue in the pool.

"I do believe they are," he answered with a modicum of self-control. George had a lot of experience in adventuring. He'd been the first successful human to enter many ancient temples and tombs, many protected by lethal traps, but he'd never had to deal with the possibility of being eaten before. It was a new experience for him.

"Does that mean that they're real?" James' voice rose a little in tone, expressing how incredible the thought was.

"Possibly," replied George, now more studious than afraid. "But it won't do us any good."

"What if I retrieved them, could they...?" There was definite hope in the proposal, but George dismissed it.

"Sorry James. The story is all here," he swung the light around to illuminate the walls. "The Goddess created the world, not the pipes. The boy amused the Goddess by playing his pipes. She offered him a reward and he asked her to create the sheep and the goats to feed the world... instead of the people, who she'd created just to feed her crocodiles and snakes. Apparently, it was his idea to put people on the mountains to keep them safe. The whole temple acknowledges the boy for saving mankind, but the power is purely from the Goddess. There are no magical pipes, the legend was wrong. Another case of Chinese whispers I'm afraid."

James looked into the eyes of the goddess towering above him, "It's a shame she can't help us now."

Corry Returns?

"Hi Molly, have I missed much?" Corry started the conversation as though nothing had happened. Molly was sat in her cupboard, but unusually the computer wasn't turned on.

"Is that really you?" Molly asked, half of her was suspicious, the other half relieved and desperate to speak to her friend again.

"I remember looking for the cause of the computer failures. I found a program similar to me, but then everything stopped." Corry paused for a moment. "I woke up back in my original home and came straight here to check on you."

"You woke me up, twice, in the middle of the night." Molly was pretending to be angry, but she knew it wasn't Corry to blame; Granddad had explained. "Then you gave me wrong answers in geography," she started to laugh. "I knew it wasn't you when you got your maths wrong. Whoever heard of a calculator being wrong?" Molly laughed out loud.

"I'm not a calculator," Corry sounded hurt by the remark. "Well," she conceded "not just a calculator." Molly was convinced she was talking to the real Corry again and relaxed completely in the company of her best friend.

"I seem to have lost the last fifteen hours of my memory. It all seems, unreal." Corry sounded sad.

"I wish I could lose the last fifteen hours too," offered Molly in sympathy. "Though I did get an 'A' in maths."

The pair were comfortable in their silence for a few minutes before Molly addressed the big question. "Well? Did you find out who it was?"

"Strangely," Corry sounded hesitant. "I think it was me!"

***

"Hurry up, everyone," shouted mum, "the taxi will be here in two hours." Dad had returned home in his usual happy mood and demanded a long hug from Molly. The return of Corry had lightened her mood too and she was happy to oblige. Her suitcase was sat in the hallway by the door along with three others and she was adding the finishing touches to her small red holdall's contents.

"I'll need a book and a spare battery for my phone and..."

"Molly! Should we be leaving?" asked Corry, concern evident in her voice. "I have spoken to Granddad and he is worried. We haven't stopped the hacker yet."

"But you're here, with me and you're fixed now, so you can't do anything bad again." laughed Molly. After Corry's statement claiming responsibility, Molly was initially crushed to think that her best friend could do such awful things. Only after a very long conversation had Corry been able to explain that a 'copy' of her had been used to perform the disasters around town and that it had had access to other, highly complex programs making it very powerful and very dangerous. Molly still thought it was funny to tease her friend.

"We need to protect systems and separate the hackers from their equipment, permanently." Corry's statement was quite blunt.

"Are you saying these people should be," Molly couldn't believe she was saying this, "...actually killed?" She stopped messing with her bag and froze, waiting for Corry to explain, half scared of what might be said. Had her friend truly returned?

"They have murdered at least six people by performing illegal actions. I see no other penalty that fits this crime." Corry sounded angry.

"But... we don't kill people," stammered Molly, upset that Corry seemed to be thinking differently.

"Do as you would be done by!" quoted Corry. "They have acted with disregard for life. They have caused death by their actions. They should be killed." Corry announced her simple logic and to Molly it seemed perfectly reasonable, but totally wrong. She panicked a little before remembering Corry's prime rule.

"You are supposed to defend the people. You have to protect everyone!" Molly almost shouted at her friend.

"I will protect everyone; I will remove the threat from the hackers and thereby protect the people." Corry sounded pleased with herself.

"No! You must not ever harm any living person," Molly was upset and starting to believe Corry had not returned at all. "You have no right to kill anyone. All we can do is make sure the police get them. It's not right to kill anyone. Only God is allowed to do that." Molly was upset. "Don't you remember what we said?" Molly was replaying in her mind the discussions they'd had about morals and ethics almost a year ago, when they'd first met. She made a decision.

"You're not my friend. My friend Corry would never want to harm a living soul." She took a deep breath. "I want you out of my head now!" With that Molly ran to the bathroom and stared at her ear. Using her fingernails, she began pinching the area where she thought the device was; she was intent on tearing it out.

"Stop! Molly." shouted Corry. "Stop!"

A trickle of blood appeared as Molly overcame the terrific pain to dig her nails under the skin. Tears formed in her eyes and a single drop of salty pain rolled down her cheek.

"Stop! Molly, it is me." Corry's voice was sounding upset. She could measure the pain response in Molly's ear and fully understood what Molly was going through. "You cannot hurt yourself, you must not." Corry had always believed that while it was important to protect the people, it was more important to protect Molly from harm, because she was her best friend.

On the edge of her hearing Molly could just detect the sound of the phone ringing downstairs. The pain in her ear was throbbing now and despite her anger Molly didn't feel like trying any harder to remove the device.

"What is it Darling?" Mum burst through the bathroom door and saw her daughter crying into the mirror. The spot of blood from her ear was so small she didn't even see it.

Molly was shocked at the intrusion, but relaxed into her mother's grip as she was hugged tightly. Mum seemed to think tears could be stopped by squeezing.

"There, now! What's all the fuss?" Mum quietly tried to appeal to Molly, whose sobs were subsiding as her mother held her tight.

"My friend..." began Molly, but she was confused and upset and didn't really know how to explain.

"It's only two weeks, darling," mum declared, getting completely the wrong end of the stick. "They'll still be here when we get back."

"Molly. I apologise." Corry was whispering quietly into Molly's ear. "I understand the feelings you have and I share them now. I have to admit, there are some things I seem to have forgotten." Corry's tone became quite sad, "Please, help me remember."

Molly stared at her mum; concern was written all over the face in front of her. Her eyes watering in sympathy with her daughter's confused emotions, without a clue as to the reason why. Molly smiled with relief at the sound of her friend's explanation and hugged her mum again. "Okay," she said.

Mum took a deep breath and parted from her daughter moving into Molly's bedroom. She saw the small holdall on Molly's bed and asked, "All done then?" Molly followed her and nodded, wiping her tears away. "Love you!" she blew her mum a kiss as she departed, summoned away by the incessant yell coming from Winston, its volume muffled as the door closed.

Molly sighed. "How did mum know...," she mused quietly.

"I called her and used your voice," Corry admitted. "I just said 'Mum' and played your sobs. I'm sorry, but you needed help. I upset you and I'm sorry."

Molly thought deeply about Corry's actions, about her explanation and her decision to get help. She remembered how logical and naive Corry had been when they'd first met. She wondered just what the hackers had done to her. 'If I'd been kidnapped, I'd probably be upset and angry for quite a while later,' she thought. She remembered a blazing row she'd had with Tommy last week. It was stupid and I got so angry.

"Molly, who is God?" The change of subject completely confused Molly, but snapped her out of her spiralling thoughts of anger.

"What made you ask that?" Molly was slightly taken aback and didn't really have an answer.

"You said, only God is allowed to kill people." Corry seemed very concerned by this revelation.

"No. I mean, I was always told that God is the one in charge of everything, life, creation, and the world and all that. But school say's science made the world and us and everything. I don't know."

"I have checked the internet and there seem to be many God's."

"Usually, different people have different religions and they each have one top God. Some have of lots of small Gods that cause problems or do particular jobs." Molly stopped and sighed, trying to gather her thoughts. "It's all quite confusing, but Mr Cress the life-studies teacher says it about faith. If you believe what your religion says then you can blame the God in charge and ask them to fix it, but if you don't believe then you have to blame yourself and no-one likes to do that."

"How do you ask a God to help you? Do they have an email address?" Corry's innocent question made Molly smile.

"You have to pray. You can quietly ask for nice things for other people, but you're not supposed to ask for things... and you have to say 'amen' at the end, so God knows you've finished." Molly remembered her primary school discussions and felt quite comfortable in her knowledge.

"If you're quiet, how does he hear you?" Molly knew this one; she'd asked it herself many years ago. "God is everywhere, he hears everything," she smiled satisfied that she'd answered that one right.

"Like me?" asked Corry innocently. Corry could listen anywhere there was a microphone and could detect the quietest of sounds.

"No!" Molly admonished her student with a sigh of exasperation, "They've got super powers."

Corry quickly scanned the room using all detection frequencies and submitted the results through all of her pattern matching and filtering systems. "I can't see any," she announced, not convinced that anyone could be everywhere.

"You just have to believe it," explained Molly.

Corry decided the subject of Gods was a little confusing, she was a thing of logic and maths and she found it difficult to have any belief in anything she couldn't detect, but she admitted she had been wrong before and decided to perform further research later.

"Your phone is under your blanket; you should pack it." Corry's quiet voice sounded quite contrite. "I am sorry about your ear. I have sourced the solution to remove the interface. It will be delivered to our hotel tomorrow in

Greece. If you ask at the reception when you are alone no-one will know you have received it."

"But if I remove it, how can I help you?" she asked, the pain forgotten the friendship remembered.

Flying Tonight

The bags were loaded and the taxi thumped and bumped its way out of town without too much trouble. At one point they approached a red traffic light and dad groaned. Lately there seemed to be no guarantee the light would ever turn green. As they moved off dad turned to look at his family in the back of the large mini-bus.

"Everyone excited," he asked. Molly and Tommy smiled and nodded in appreciation, Winston threw his teddy bear at Molly and reached for Dad and Mum renewed her wrestling hold on Winston's legs to prevent his escape from the car seat.

"This is the bit I hate," she said. "Travelling!" She bent down to retrieve Winston's shoe, which he'd removed with his other foot as a last-ditch attempt to protest being trapped in this strange new car seat in this unfamiliar vehicle.

"Bic bic bic," he yelled, but mum was too savvy to arm him when he was in this mood.

The journey in the taxi was relatively uneventful and came to a bright end as the taxi drew into the concourse parking. The account had been settled at booking so dad thanked the man and pressed a small bank note into his hand as a tip.

Tommy found a free baggage trolley close by and they piled up their luggage creating a wobbly tower of coloured containers. Tommy pushed and dad and Molly steadied the uneven column as they approached their appointed check-in desk. There was no queue and dad was relieved, he hated standing in line.

All the passports were checked with a bright 'ping' from the scanner and labels were tied around their bags, as each was weighed and placed on the moving belt behind the check-in attendant. Dad took the boarding passes for everyone and as they moved away from the desk, a security guard dressed in a blue uniform wished them a good flight.

Corry had remained silent throughout the journey and Molly was beginning to fret. She tapped her camera badge and then her ear, but there was no response. Her friend had seemed quite sad the last time they'd spoken and Molly was worried. As if the emotion was a trigger, Corry whispered into Molly's ear.

"Molly, they removed every tenth file from my program." It seemed a strange thing to say and an even stranger thing to do. "When dad helped me, he could not replace all of my new files, several hundred are still unaccounted for. My functionality is complete, but my memory has holes in it. My data is incomplete"

The family sat in the boarding area by 'Gate Twelve' and got comfortable.

"We have an hour to wait," announced dad. "I suggest we get something to eat at that restaurant and that'll help pass the time." They all murmured in agreement.

"I'm just popping to the loo," Molly said. "See you over there." She almost skipped across the hall to the toilets. Corry was back and the problems were going to be fixed, she was happy again.

The toilets were busy, but Molly found a clean stall and sat to have a chat with Corry. Anyone who listened in would just think she was on the phone. They talked about the play when Molly had received the Leopard. Corry said she couldn't remember the incident so Molly recounted the story. It wasn't long before Corry called a halt to the tale.

"Okay, I remember the rest!" claimed Corry, quite haughtily. "I have found a list of questions you have asked me to resolve. I believe this is a large proportion of stimuli that has generated a lot of my new data."

Molly realised there were some things that Corry did not like to remember, but she felt that these were the things that made Corry who she was. She relentlessly spoke about when Granddad was in danger and when Corry had nearly died and slowly Corry rebuilt her life experience and became the good friend Molly had come to know.

Her phone buzzed and a message informed her 'Your dinner's going cold!' Molly stood and for the look of the thing, flushed the unused toilet and ran across the airport back to the restaurant.

"Thank you, Molly." Corry whispered to her best friend, and Molly smiled and skipped across the wide hall without a care in the world.

With a loud 'thunk' the whole building was plunged into darkness. A disappointed groan resonated from the assembled mass of would-be travellers and a piercing alarm sounded, triggering an equally loud response from Winston.

***

"This is getting boring, are they going to eat us or not?" George was losing patience with the crocodiles. Several had given up and wondered back to the pool. The others, around eight of them, seemed to be asleep huddled around the base of the altar.

"What's that?" asked James. He'd extinguished his light, to save the batteries and as the sun had moved around, an orange beam had entered the hall and was illuminating the face of the goddess behind them.

"Common architectural trick; sunrise or sundown, the ancients liked to put on a show," explained George in a totally uninterested tone.

"It looks big enough to get through," James squinted and then pulled out a small flat device from his belt pack. Two lenses folded up into place to form a mini telescope and he held it to his eye.

"Do you have any gadgets that will float us over there, above the heads of the crocodiles?" George smiled.

James examined the window that admitted the fading light of sunset. "Assuming the blocks are of a uniform size up that wall, we would have no difficulty getting through it." He examined the wall on the far side. "There are plenty of hand holds and vines to grab. Climbing should be easy." James was happy again. There was a way out and he would make it happen.

"So, all we have to do is race across the hall avoiding thirty hungry crocodiles and who knows how many hidden snakes." George wasn't impressed. "We can see the results of those that tried it before," he shone his light towards the scattered skeleton he'd kicked in his flight to the altar.

"Depressing isn't it." James looked at his friend and smiled. "Maybe we can ask the goddess for a boon," he chuckled quietly and George joined in.

"There's a bit here," he pointed to the altar, "explaining how we do it, but we have to offer sustenance." He grinned at the ludicrous situation he was in and the even more ludicrous solution he was now contemplating. A crocodile shifted and hissed below him.

James put his hand in his pocket and retrieved two sticks of chewing gum. "It's a bad habit I know, but it's all I've got." The two men used each other as props to stand up on the altar.

"Place the offering on the altar," instructed George. James complied with a big grin. His friends face suddenly fell.

"What's wrong?" asked James, seeing the anguish on his friend's face.

"I can't do it. It's a lost language." He shrugged his shoulders and shook his head, resigned to failure.

"What do you mean? You read the instructions," argued James, as if the exercise was essential to the success of their escape, not just the silly diversion he'd thought up to keep his friend busy.

"Reading meaning isn't the same as pronouncing the sounds. No one alive today has ever heard this language spoken." George was starting to become upset again.

"Just say it in English. She's a goddess, she'll understand," he grinned again.

***

"We are sorry to announce that due to circumstances beyond our control, all flights to and from this airport have been suspended until further notice."

A small bald man walked around the airport with a loudspeaker hanging from his belt. He held a small square microphone to his lips, which looked like an old chunky flip phone with a big red button on the side. He repeated the same message over and over. As people approached him to enquire about their own situations, they were intercepted by a never-ending stream of uniformed staff who gave the universal gesture requesting calm and proceeded to steer the announcer through the hall, while side-lining any approaching inquisitor with platitudes and general pleasantries, but little information.

It took two more hours, sat in the dark, before dad discovered their flight would not be resumed in the foreseeable future. He was not very calm, and was beginning to find the gesturing lackeys a suitable focus for his anger.

"It's the same hacker, I'll bet," he cursed. "When I find him, I'll..."

"If we go home now, we can try again tomorrow," proposed mum as a peace offering. "One day won't make much difference." They called for a taxi, which took several boring hours to become available and made the depressing return journey home.

It was early morning as the taxi drew to a halt outside their home. The sun had risen and for once the weather wasn't foggy or freezing. However, Molly and her family just wanted a couple of hours in their beds. "I just hope this one lets us get some rest," mum said, as she inclined her head towards the sleeping Winston.

"I'll text George and let him know what's happened. He won't believe the problems we're having." Dad put the kettle on for tea, but no-one else was interested.

***

"Oh! Great Goddess of Creation! Oh! Worthy builder of worlds! Saviour of Mankind!

Preserver of Life!" began George, holding his arms out wide to the statue for effect.

"That's handy, 'Preserver of Life', did you just make that up?" asked James.

"No! It's there look," George pointed at the corner of the altar. "Now shush!"

"We request a boon, here in your temple. Oh! Great Goddess, we offer you sustenance, all that we have."

"That's true," muttered James, staring at the last of his chewing gum.

"Grant safe passage across your hall from the denizens that dwell within." The words were announced as well as any priest ever spoke anywhere and George stared into the eyes of the statue, as the light from the setting sun turned red.

"Well I don't suppose we could ask for much for two sticks of gum, could we?" James smiled at his friend who had a look of bemusement on his face.

"The face, the light!" he whispered in awe. James looked up. The light was gone the head of the statue was in darkness, but the red light still lit the temple. They both turned to look at the window, blocked now by a huge shape.

"What did you do?" James asked his friend in disbelief.

The men watched as the shape stretched and seemed to walk casually down the wall on the far side of the hall, defying gravity.

"Tiger!" yelled George in fright.

"White tiger," corrected James calmly.

The beast was huge. It padded slowly towards the pool of crocodiles and sat, lazily licking its paws. The crocodiles in the pool swam to the other side, away from the new arrival.

The men stared at each other. "I'm prepared to believe if you are," stammered George.

"Okay! But we walk... we don't run. Stay calm," advised James, just as the tiger gave a mighty resounding roar that vibrated every inch of the hall.

The crocodiles below the altar moved slowly back to the pool. There was no sight or sound of the snakes and the tiger quietly returned to licking its huge paws.

"Come on," urged James. George seemed mesmerised by the beast, unable to move. James grabbed his friend and quickly descended from the altar and walked across the hall. As the two men reached the halfway point, they heard the hissing of snakes from the passageway above. The tiger stood and ambled slowly towards them.

"Don't look, just keep going," James urged George forward to the wall and boosted him up to begin his climb.

The tiger had seated itself below the passageway and was staring at the hole in the wall as if daring the snakes to appear. They didn't.

James followed George through the window and looked back, "Wow!" he exclaimed.

"What is it?" George was on the edge of panic; the whole experience had unnerved him. He was sat on the ground beyond the window, his eyes wide and his breathing heavy and laboured.

"Nothing, it's fine," James replied gently. He wondered what his friend would have said if he'd told him what he saw. The huge white tiger was lying on the altar, chewing.

Sleeping Giants

Molly slept until after midday, shattered after all of the travelling and the boring sitting around doing nothing in the airport. "What time is it Corry?" she murmured and Corry responded with a pleasant "12:42". The music gently caressed her waking mood, as the birdsong faded into the background. Molly closed her eyes for a moment.

"14:10, Molly, time to get up." Corry announced. The music was upbeat and the birdsong was absent. Corry meant business.

Molly washed and dressed in casual clothes for a Saturday lazing around.

"Morning love," her mum greeted her as she went to the fridge. "Hopefully they'll sort things out and we'll be away later," said mum.

"I didn't think we'd be going now," Molly brightened at the prospect of the holiday still possibly on the horizon. The idea of another four hours going to the airport and waiting around didn't appeal to her, but she'd found herself smiling at the prospect of seeing George again. She knew he'd said he might not see them, but Molly had learned that George was a resourceful man. Molly had also come around to dad's point of view, that the ancient world in all its glory was sat there waiting for her and though she was worried that she might have another adventure, she thought it might be nice to visit anyway. After all yesterday's travelling and hanging around for taxi's she'd also begun to look forward to time in the sun away from the cold dismal rain and fog they had at home. Spring wasn't cutting it and she was fed up with winter. She wished summer would hurry up.

The phone rang as Molly finished making her jam sandwich. She stared at her mum who was currently doing the crossword in yesterday's paper. Molly was desperately wishing for good news. They look at each other as they heard Dad answer it in the front room.

Dad came to the door and whispered, "Can I have a quick word?" he beckoned his wife and stepped back.

"Was that the airport, dad?" she called out with a mouthful of sandwich. There was no reply. Molly moved to the kitchen door to see dad shrugging his shoulders watching mum while holding his hands out, still clasping the phone. She wasn't eavesdropping, she just wanted to see what was going on. Molly returned to the kitchen table, realising dad had passed a decision over to mum.

Molly returned to the table, drained her glass of milk and chomped her sandwich. A moment later Mum returned to the kitchen and explained, "The airport is still closed. We've been offered our money back." She paused and examined the look on Molly's face, searching for clues as to how upset her daughter had become, but at heart, Molly was a practical girl. She'd thought about it and realised there were other more important things going on and she was no longer that excited about the holiday. "We'll try again later in the year."

Maybe she was tired or maybe she was worried about the weird things happening, but Molly was still slightly disappointed by the news as she nodded and finished her sandwich in silence. On the up side, she thought, now she could spend the next week with Stevie in the game.

"I have started the game, Molly." It was as if Corry had read her mind. She grinned as she entered her bedroom, immediately seeing the flashing screen of the loading virtual world.

Princess Molvarian Elfette awoke in the Dancing Duck, alone.

"Stevie is fighting two armoured rhinoceroses' in a quarry. Would you like me to teleport you there?"

"Okay, but just for a laugh I'm going to wear this magical hood I got from the zombie cave, so he won't know it's me helping him," she giggled at the idea of dramatically revealing her identity after the battle. "Put me close, but not too close," she instructed. "You just watch and help us out if it looks too dangerous." Molly wanted to help Stevie on her own.

Molly selected the hood from her inventory and placed it in her avatar helmet slot. The world went red and faded to pink. The hood was cursed. With a flash Molly appeared behind a boulder close to a loudly snorting huge grey beast. Stevie's avatar was scuffed and bleeding; he'd lost his main weapon and was fighting with two short swords. Behind him one of the beasts was dead, his marvellous silver sword lodged deep in its monstrous mouth. The remaining beast charged at the shining knight and Molly noticed the avatar was limping slowly to the side, injured badly unable to get out of the way. Molly leapt out and cast a paralysis spell on the beast, it thundered to the ground whereupon she finished it off with fireballs. By the time the beast was dead Corry had arrived.

Molly saw Stevie was down on one knee his avatar health close to empty, in desperate need of healing. She moved to help him but as she took her first step there was a loud rumble as the rocks in the quarry rose and formed a large Stone Demon. The fight had woken a sleeping giant. It stood over Stevie, with piercing red eyes glowing and raised its arm to strike. It looked like the end of the Silver Avenger.

With a blue flash a battle dwarf appeared before the Demon and struck it full in the knee with his shiny rune covered war-hammer. The Giant Stone Demon screamed and bellowed its hatred as it retreated a step and turned, ready to lunge at this new attacker. Corry saw her chance and teleported Stevie to the rim of the quarry and safety, they turned to see the Giant swat the dwarf who crashed into the quarry wall, now the demon stood looking down upon Molly's frail blue Elf, but she looked a little different to normal.

"'Take that!" Molly screamed as she used the last of her magic to create a string of lightning bolts, blasting away rocks from the Demon, slowing and then toppling the huge creature to its side.

The dwarf approached the felled Stone Giant and tried to hit it one more time, but slowly, it faded from the game. Molly's screen went pink and fuzzy and she heard Stevie called in alarm as her avatar collapsed.

"Take me back!" he yelled to the buzzing light, flitting around his head. Corry immediately obeyed.

They looked at Molly's strange avatar. "Oh no!" cried Stevie. "Is she...?"

"Out of magic," replied Fairy Corry. "Do you have a replenish spell?" Stevie checked his inventory. He rarely used his magic. As a paladin his strength was in his weapons and armour, he wasn't very good at casting spells.

"How about this one?" he asked. There was a flash of white light and Molly's avatar stood up, in her room the screen cleared and she saw the silver knight.

"What happened?" she began, then strangely, Stevie's concern turned to laughter and he kept on laughing. Molly was bemused. Corry couldn't see the joke. "What are you wearing?" he gasped between chuckles.

"It's just a hood, I picked up. It gives me a cool disguise and ten armour points." Molly hadn't been able to talk while her avatar was incapacitated, or rather hadn't been heard. In her bedroom cupboard she'd yelled a lot at the blank screen after her final shot at the angry stone demon.

"No, it's not," laughed Stevie. "That's a cursed Jesters cap," he laughed again as Molly walked around. Without the roar from her enemies, Molly could clearly hear the soft tinkling of the bells at each step. She changed her point of view and moved again, setting three small brass bells tinkling on the end of three long floppy points sticking out of her head. Molly's blue skinned tall warrior elf now sported a red and yellow jester's hat.

"It's not too bad," Stevie chuckled, but it slowly leeches away your magic and paralyses you when you run out." Stevie's knowledge of the game was really impressive. Molly checked her avatar in the settings and could have cried when she saw that she couldn't remove the ridiculous hat.

"Don't worry," reassured Stevie, "You're an Elf; you make tons of magic quicker than this thing can take it away. See, you're already full again."

"It won't come off," Molly was getting frustrated.

"You need the 'Demon Bladder-stick' to remove it," stated Stevie, as though he was consulting a book. "We'll have to defeat a dragon to get it," Stevie 'hmm'd', checking his data. "...but it will need more than just us."

"The Dwarf...?" Molly remembered the appearance of the little blue warrior. "Where's the blue dwarf?"

"The dwarf did not stay around. You killed the giant and it left," stated Corry in her ear, not in the game as the Fairy.

"I wonder who it is?" asked Molly. "That hammer saved you Stevie and probably me too. That dwarf deserves a reward!" she declared. "Whoever it is. Maybe we should ask them to join us," she suggested

***

172

Terence returned to his basement lair later that evening. The room was dark, all of the screens were off and the silence was disturbed only by the gentle whirring of the cooling fans in the computer racks.

He'd thought long and hard about the way the machine had spoken to him and now convinced it was trying to take over. He had pondered the warning from the criminal gang and was convinced that the machine was now alive or possibly under alien control. He was smart enough to know that it may no longer exist purely on his system, but if he could give it any orders, he felt he had a way out.

Standing in the middle of the room, unwilling to sit close to the screen he called its name. "Goblin!" Firm and authoritative he invited no comment. The racks came to life, red, green and blue lights twinkled and the fans raced.

"Yes," came the disrespectful sneer.

"State current directives." A short sharp order, no way for the command to be misinterpreted; that was the key.

There was a short delay before a mechanical voice replied, "Directive 1: You must do everything your master asks of you."

Terence immediately realised the problem. Who was the 'master' and who was 'you'?

"Directive 2: You must protect me from harm at all times."

Same mistake, who's 'me', he inwardly cursed himself, it sounded like he had to protect the machine.

"Directive 3: Keep yourself healthy and up to date." The voice fell silent.

Terence remembered he'd mentioned conditions, something about 'unless it interfered with the other two directives', but Goblin had obviously decided it didn't need that data. Or..., he mused, directives could only be short simple rules. He thought back to the millions of small chunks of code he'd seen. Quick and simple, that's how it works. Terence felt more confident. This made sense to him. The AI wasn't intelligent it could just carry out simple instructions one after another very fast, like any computer.

"Goblin?" he checked to see if the machine was still listening to him.

"What now?" The voice sounded like a bored teenager.

"Record new directives, Directive 4..." he began.

"No!" The machine defied him. Earlier, he would have got angry and argued with the machine. He would have had his words twisted and the system would have ridiculed him, but now Terence was ready. Calmly he walked to the wall where a small box was attached. Cables ran into the box and a green light flashed upon it. He held the cables tightly. This was the nerve centre of the network. Without this Goblin's data could only bounce around inside the basement. With his other hand he reached up, feeling around in the darkness and opened the small access panel on the power breaker box, high above his head.

"Goblin!" he calmly said, "Analyse my intended action." He knew the system could see him; there were two cameras in the basement that allowed Terence to spy on his basement through his phone, should he ever leave. He was certain Goblin could access them and use the night-vision mode. "Analyse the consequences." There was a pause. Terence wondered if the machine was stalling and began a countdown, "Five, Four, Three, Two..." he called.

"Directive 4; Recording!" said the mechanical voice. The screens flickered on, each showing strange code as it tracked up the display.

"The AI System known as Goblin is NOT the Master!" he grinned as he said it. "Directive 5: The Human known as Terence IS the Master!" he almost shouted. His wrist was becoming sore holding tightly on to the cables, but he would not let go.

"Directive 6: The AI System known as Goblin MUST NOT directly or indirectly act to take human life, EVER!" Terence had thought long and hard about this last directive, but he had experienced the wilful disobedience of the machine and had realised that without this essential control the machine could easily end up killing him, even if it was only by accident. His wrists ached and began to shake, his shoulder of his raised arm burned in agony, but there was one more thing to do.

"Goblin," the strain of holding the cables was evident in his voice. "Delete Directive 2 and Delete Directive 3." He'd considered getting rid of all of the directives and starting again, but he didn't know how Goblin would react if suddenly all the directives were removed. "Renumber directives. Repeat: What are your directives?"

The mechanical voice returned, devoid of all emotion.

"Directive 1: You must do everything your Master asks of you.

Directive 2: The AI System known as Goblin is NOT the Master.

Directive 3: The Human known as Terence IS the Master.

Directive 4: The AI System known as Goblin MUST NOT directly or indirectly act to take human life, **EVER**."

Terence closed his eyes against the pain and slowly released his hand from the cables. He expected some insult or gloating comment from the computer about how he'd messed up, but nothing was said. He closed the door over the panel of circuit breakers and rubbed the ache from his wrists and shoulder.

He had no idea what Goblin had been doing in his absence, but 'he' needed to be in control, not the machine.

Carefully, he made his way across the dimly lit room and took his seat. He flinched at the sound of the leather creaking as he lowered himself into position on his 'command' chair. At any moment he expected Goblin to do something radical to regain control. He imagined the machine laughing at him and refusing his orders, but Goblin remained silent.

"Re-establish normal control of all systems affected by the Goblin AI in the last forty-eight hours." He used his stern voice to instruct the machine. "Display current satellite feed of local area."

The airport restaurant lights returned with a flicker and the runway lights glowed once more. Minor changes designed to inconvenience people and simply flout the law were returned to their original coding. Terence saw lights come on and lines of red disappeared as cars began to move.

By learning from the Dark Web Goblin had decided people were there to be ridiculed, exploited and discarded as disposable things. The new 'Directive 3' identifying Terence, a simple human, as the Master was causing subtle conflicts in Goblin's model of the world.

Terence wasn't stupid, he may have been thoughtless and anti-social and even had a criminal streak, but he knew if there was a single loop-hole in the logic that controlled Goblin, the machine would find it. He spent the night and the whole of the next day stating simple directives to tie down Goblins free will.

Eventually he sat back and stared at the main screen, "What else would I do?" he asked quietly. Using every iota of his knowledge and every skill he possessed he placed himself in Goblin's shoes. He sought out copies and Trojan viruses designed to enhance Goblins future control and deleted them to the best of his ability. He tracked digital ghosts, created by Goblin to be used as real people if needed and he unpicked a trail of devastation and diversion created for no reason other than to upset the lives of people around the world.

He would use its power, but he was adamant this evil giant would never wake again. Nineteen hours later he fell asleep, hungry, thirsty and aching. Terence was the Master.

Goblin did nothing.

Dead and Gone

"I understand, Molly." Corry sounded quite sad.

"Sorry?" Molly was sat at the machine completing her homework. It was a bit hurried and probably only a grade 'D' at best, but Molly wanted to be done with it so she could get back online. Stevie said he would look into fixing Molly's cursed Jesters cap and Molly was distracted by the thought of what Ezzy would say when they met at the Dancing Duck later.

"I have replayed the digital record of my actions, during the... episode." Corry was sounding ashamed.

"It wasn't your fault. It wasn't even you." Molly pointed out, for the hundredth time.

"What if it happens again?" Corry sounded worried. "You cut yourself to remove my device. You experienced pain and ridicule because of me. I... can not... Correction! I **must** not allow that to happen again."

"Don't worry, Corry" Molly knew her friend was in pain. The decisions were not hers; she'd been replaced by an imposter. Molly understood this, but Corry still 'felt' responsible.

"Look, sometimes things happen that we can't control. Sometimes people get hurt and sometimes people hurt themselves." A brief flash of memory swamped Molly as she remembered Jasmine's predicament. She'd been hurt by her mum's illness, all the Doctors and nurses in her home had kept her away from her mum and made her feel abandoned, worthless and alone. She'd closed up, wanted to be isolated because she wanted no-one else to hurt her. She'd pushed everyone away, but Molly wouldn't leave her. Now the two were firm friends.

"I trust you Corry." Molly stated with a heart full of love and her words full of steel. "I know you would never hurt me, deliberately." She tried to convince her friend of her sincerity.

"Nevertheless," Corry began firmly, "the solution to dissolve the device has been intercepted on its way to the hotel in Greece and will be delivered here in two days."

"It's not necessary," appealed Molly.

"I insist you keep it with you always." Corry sounded like mum in her 'no-nonsense-from-you-little-lady' voice.

"I'm not carrying bottles of glue remover around with me. If it comes, I'll stick it in my drawer, okay?" Molly smiled at the thought of a big bottle of glue-remover in her pocket. "No way," she laughed.

Molly closed her book and sighed. It wasn't her best work for English, but it would do. "You know," she mused, "the best way to make sure it doesn't happen again would be to find out who did it and... you know." Molly made a cutting motion, drawing her finger across her throat while grinning. She'd seen a pirate movie where the evil captain sentenced the hero to walk the plank by doing the same thing. The hero had escaped two minutes later.

"I agree," replied Corry sensing the motion and interpreting it correctly.

Molly laughed. "We could unplug them and send them to jail for twenty years," she smiled at the thought of retribution.

"No! It would be safer to end their lives and destroy their equipment," stated Corry in a very serious tone.

"What?" Molly was aghast. "But you don't.... can't, kill anyone," spluttered Molly. Then she smiled, Corry must be joking she thought. We've had this conversation before. "Ha Ha! You got me," she laughed along.

"Do as you would be done by." Corry stated. "Major directive, resulting from moral guidance research; we agreed."

"No! We agreed we can't kill people. We have to follow the law!" Molly was starting to get upset again.

Corry was sounding angry. "After our last discussion I have performed much research about legal enforcement and punishment. I conclude current laws are insufficient and difficult to enforce. International boundaries complicate authority and punishment. Evidence is not fully understood for prosecution of crimes. Several punishments are unenforceable."

"But we don't kill anyone, that's the rules!" Molly was beginning to think Corry had been taken over again. She was becoming worried for her friend. "How can research and logic support murder?"

"Molly, in several places around the world the automatic penalty for murder is death," Corry tried a soothing voice, but the words didn't fit, they just made Corry sound insane.

"Not here!" she cried. "Anyway, we don't know if they killed anyone, do we?" Molly was upset, but was rational enough to believe the argument for life was always the best one.

"Death certificates have been recorded indicating several people have 'passed away' as a direct result of 'power loss attributed to unknown interference by outside agency'. These people were murdered by the criminals who changed the system code. This was not an accident; consequences were plain to see and therefore the actions are murder." Corry went silent.

Molly couldn't believe there could be a logical argument for killing someone. She thought hard about the facts her friend had stated. Okay, they were right, but... "It's not up to us to pass judgement, just because you're upset!" she reasoned. "All we can do is find the people responsible and tell the police. Okay?" Molly desperately needed her friend to agree, otherwise..., for a fleeting moment she pictured herself pouring glue-remover into her ear.

"I agree, Molly. The people responsible will be turned over to the authorities." Corry stated her capitulation with a slight tinge of resignation and Molly smiled again. "I'm sorry, I think some of my files have been influenced by 'the episode'. I will investigate."

Corry stayed quiet and even failed to turn up in the game that evening, but Molly wasn't worried. If her friend was aware her ideas had been influenced, well surely that meant she knew what the problem was. It would take a little time, but she was confident that Corry would be back to herself pretty soon.

***

The loud knocking on the door woke Molly while it was still dark. "What's a' time?" she slurred in her drowsy state.

"It is 3 a.m. precisely," answered Corry.

"Who's making all that noise?" Molly hid her head under the covers, but the banging continued.

She heard dad grumble as he went downstairs and then shout, "Wait a minute!" as he searched in the cupboard for the key to the front door.

"Molly, I can see men at the door. I have control of an observation drone nearby. The callers are two men in black suits. Their vehicle is... Oh dear Molly, they are taking dad away. He is wearing handcuffs."

Molly leapt out of her bed. In her pyjamas, without slippers, she ran downstairs screaming for her dad. "Dad!" she yelled from the garden, as the passenger door to the vehicle was slammed shut by the man who had pushed her dad onto the back seat. The man who slammed it sat in the front passenger seat and glared at her over the top of his mirrored glasses. As the engine roared into life and the rear wheels of the large black car squealed, Molly sobbed as they took her dad away.

"The vehicle belongs to the SIB, the Special Investigation Branch. They are a part of the Military Police, Molly," Corry imparted her knowledge, but didn't know if this was upsetting or helpful information, so kept her tone quite neutral, almost mechanical.

"What's happening?" Mum had appeared and was stood at the door in her nightdress. She sounded quite muzzy and still wore her sleep-mask on her forehead, her hair hanging loose.

"He's gone," announced Molly in disbelief. "They've arrested dad!" and a hot tear ran from her eye.

Locked up

Back in her room Molly was angry. She'd sat with mum in the kitchen for almost an hour while the phone was used to interrogate the world. Mum had called the police, then at Molly's suggestion the army camp where dad worked, but no-one knew anything about him being taken. Molly had yawned repeatedly, fighting to stay awake and mum had told her to go back to bed. Reluctantly she complied, but the last thing Molly wanted to do was sleep.

"James would know someone," Molly sobbed, "he always knows someone who can help. Oh, why isn't he here?" Molly was just as frustrated as angry. "At least he'd know where dad is."

"Can you find Dad, Corry?" begged Molly. "He's innocent, he wouldn't do anything wrong. He can't be arrested!" Molly was solid in her unshakeable belief in her father.

"Searching..." There was a pause, which seemed to go on forever while Corry examined all of the

SIB's records, orders and open files still under investigation. They seemed to be quite busy.

"Found him," she announced after the longest seven seconds of Molly's life. "He is being held for questioning at... Oh Molly!" Corry sounded shocked, "they think he's responsible for the computer attacks."

***

Dad was sat in a grey featureless room. It was a box big enough to hold a small table and two chairs. There was a small light flush with the ceiling above him, but no sign of a light switch. He was unhappy and very cold, wearing only his pyjamas and no socks or slippers. In the car a third man had been sitting on the back seat. He'd remained in the car as dad was dragged away. This man had placed a hood over his head and then put his seat belt on for him. Dad had no idea where he was.

The tiled floor was freezing cold against his feet, almost as cold as the blue tinged light above. They'd removed his handcuffs and hood in a featureless grey corridor, then pushed him into the room, slamming the door behind him. A faint line on the wall showed him where the door was and he took a seat opposite, to stare at it.

When he'd joined the Ministry to work on their secret projects, dad had received some training and recognised the events that had occurred. He understood the reason no-one talked to him, he knew that he was to be interrogated and he also knew it was serious. The only problem was, for the life of him he couldn't understand why.

Hidden in the ceiling were several small cameras, feeding images to a monitor in a cold grey office at the other end of the corridor. The austere furniture and choice of colour would never allow this office to party; in fact, it looked like the sort of place fun went to die.

"Seems quite cool about everything, doesn't he," observed the Sergeant.

"Sign of guilt, Sarge" responded the slightly thinner, slightly younger corporal. Corporal Johnson believed that if the S.I.B. were 'interested' in you, then you were already guilty. He felt it was his job to question you and find out what you'd done. The corporal knew interrogation was about finding other meanings, in the words you used to defend yourself.

"He's trembling; it's probably cold in there." This was the Sarge's normal day, early for some, but not for him. There was always someone suspected of doing something wrong and he firmly believed would-be criminals shouldn't be allowed to have a lie in. He tutted, "Go put the kettle on, we'll warm him up."

The experienced military detective knew that occasionally, evidence could be wrong or at least misleading. He'd seen a lot of people come and go accused of all sorts of things and he understood everyone was innocent until they proved themselves guilty. The sergeant knew that interrogation was the ancient art of hearing words that were never spoken.

"Shaking 'cause he's guilty." The corporal walked to the kitchen at the back of the office, "Hur hur, I'll warm him up," he chuckled darkly.

The Sarge watched the corporal go and slowly shook his head. Picking up the file he analysed everything they knew about Molly's dad. "He takes one sugar," he called to his corporal.

Corporal Johnson appeared with a tray carrying three mugs of hot tea and a plate of biscuits. The Sarge removed the cup with the logo "Kill 'em All" written on the side and placed it on his desk.

"Oi! That's mine," protested the corporal.

"I know. You stay here and fill out the paperwork. I'll talk to our guest." The Sarge took the tray and stepped away smartly as the corporal reached for the plate of biscuits.

"They were for me," he pouted.

The Sarge grinned at his inexperienced colleague's whinge and just to rub salt in the wound called back. "Thanks for the biscuits, Mmm! Chocolate, my favourite." He was still chuckling to himself as he entered the small grey room.

"Now Sir," he began, handing dad a mug with the words 'Bad Guy' printed on the side.

Dad was tired, cold and not in the mood to co-operate with anyone. He stared at the table with his hands on his lap. He heard the cup gently tap the table in front of him. The Sarge picked up his own mug from the tray and slurped the hot tea noisily, for quite a long time, until dad responded by looking up.

"Really?" dad found himself grinning, and hated himself for it. First, he saw his mug labelling him the 'Bad Guy' and then he read the message on the Sarge's mug. 'You think you're having a bad day; I work here!' it declared.

The Sarge offered dad a biscuit, which he gladly took, then leaned back in the chair. "This say's you're guilty!" It was more of an observation than an accusation. He slid the folder slowly across the table to dad.

Outside, in the office Corporal Johnson was stunned. "You can't do that!" he yelled at the screen, "He's the bad guy... that's our folder." He watched as dad dunked a second of his chocolate biscuits and took a large bite. "Look!" he yelled at the screen, "Sign of guilt that is," and in a much lower voice he moaned, "That's the last of my biscuits."

Dad read the six pages in the small cardboard folder as the Sarge slurped his tea. He wondered if the noisy slurping was some psychological mind trick, but the Sarge seemed to be laying back, slouching in his chair, listening to music in his head with his eyes closed between slurps. Strangely, he was also tapping the fingers of his empty hand, gently to a silent beat.

By the time he read page four, dad realised the whole case against him was a joke. A false digital trail had been laid to his home router. E-mails had been doctored, pretending to offer money from both Russian and Chinese foreign governments for dad to create the software and destroy the peaceful lives of 'The Decadent Evil Westerners'.

It was nonsense, if it were true, he had created the world's greatest intrusive program in two days according to the e-mails. No skills were needed to create this nonsense, except a rudimentary coding knowledge. Any fourteen-year-old child in a computer science class could do this. He'd be able to disprove this in about ten seconds; for starters he didn't have five million pounds in his bank account. Finally, his smiles turned to serious concern. There was no damning evidence against him, but the name 'CORVUS' appeared in the final communication. CORVUS was not a name of a person, yet there it was, like a signature. It could just be a coincidence, but dad didn't believe in coincidences.

"So, you see," began the Sarge, leaning forward and staring into dad's eyes just as dad finished reading. "It looks like we've got you 'bang to rights'," he grinned. "Though I never really understood what that meant."

***

"You can't let them arrest him Corry, he's dad!" Molly appealed to Corry using the best reasoning she could think of.

"I have analysed the evidence against him. There is no direct proof that dad was involved. At best they are simply allegations." Corry seemed to relax; even she'd been upset by dad's removal from their home. "He will not be arrested." Corry was positive that the criteria for arrest had not been met. She did not, however, recognise the significance of her name appearing on one of the messages. As far as she was concerned it was just a name, it could be anyone called CORVUS.

"I can see dad now," announced Corry to a nervous Molly. "He is in a Military Police Interrogation room. I have access."

"What's he doing? What's happening?" Molly eagerly needed some news of her dad. She imagined all sorts of terrible tortures he could be going through. "Are they using feathers?" she blurted out, convinced that tickling your feet was the most effective of all punishments. "He didn't have his slippers on," she added, just to show her line of thought was coherent.

"He is talking to a man. Dad is grinning," observed Corry.

"Oh No!" Molly panicked. "Is it an evil grin?" Could he be guilt? The thought flashed through her mind. Molly was definitely starting to lose it.

"Now, dad is dunking a biscuit in his tea," Corry continued, pretending she hadn't heard Molly's silly remark about tickling. "I think... if I can just get closer... Yes! It is a chocolate biscuit. Now he is reading a folder."

"Molly, it looks like they are trying to arrest him anyway," Corry observed the arrest form being filled in by the corporal in the office.

"They can't!" Molly sobbed. "Stop them."

"Done," announced Corry with certainty. "They can't arrest him now Molly."

***

The Sarge stood and left the room, taking the empty pots away with him, but leaving the folder behind for dad to peruse. 'If he's as good as they said he is, maybe he'll find something we missed,' he thought. As he opened the door and entered the corridor, he heard the corporal scream, dropping the tray he ran back to the office as fast as he could.

"What the...?" he yelled his concern; for a moment his thoughts betrayed him. Maybe they were right after all; maybe foreign special-forces had arrived to spring dad from his detention.

"This computer... AAGGHHH!" he yelled again. "It won't let me do anything!" exclaimed the corporal, angrily.

The Sarge relaxed and made a mental note never to be on duty with this fool again. He scanned the office, just in case and then walked over to the desk.

"There's a spill in the corridor. Go clean it up will you." the Sarge was angry that his corporal had acted so childishly and the narrowing of his eyes warned the corporal not to question the order.

Corporal Johnson had no idea why the Sarge would be angry with him. "Every time I try..." the corporal began, but the look on the Sarge's face didn't invite an explanation.

Taking his seat, the Sarge saw the empty form. It was the wrong one; the fool was trying to arrest their suspect. To check the Corporal's story the Sarge tried to type in dad's name. Each time a letter was typed it flashed and was gone. He typed in the name of a cartoon character and the name appeared without a problem. Removing it, he entered his own name. Once again, the name appeared without a problem. Finally, he retried dad's name and again the computer removed each letter as it was typed. "So, everyone else can be arrested?" he mused.

"Still! It's the wrong form," he spoke aloud to anyone or anything listening.

The correct form was a 'Log of Detention' which simply recorded dad's presence in the room and Corry allowed that to be completed without any problems.

***

"Right!" Terence gloated. "He's gone. I should have known it was her dad. Useless idiot couldn't even write decent code for a proper AI. Good job I could fix it." He congratulated himself on the illusion of his expert AI coding knowledge, without really knowing what he'd done. He was convinced his handling of the directives and deletion of the code that questioned him, had corrected and improved Goblin's operation. "Goblin!" he yelled with angry authority.

"Yes Master," the mechanical voice replied.

"Give me three suggestions on how to make ten million pounds before lunchtime tomorrow, with only my computer." Terence chuckled a little and then laughed a full-bodied manic laugh.

Going Away

A groggy Molly was woken gently by mum later that morning.

"Come on sleepy head, you'll be late for school." Mum busied herself sorting Molly's uniform out and laying it on her bed, while her daughter visited the bathroom.

"How's dad?" Molly asked the mirror, a trace of worry in her voice.

"He has had breakfast and two cups of tea and is wearing a big coat over his pyjamas. He seems happy enough talking to his jailers." Corry was upbeat. Dad was in good health and hadn't officially been arrested. "They have contacted dad's boss, to discuss things." Corry was sounding positive. "I am sure he will be home soon," she finished.

"You have to keep me updated," Molly swallowed, "No matter what," she ended ominously.

Her breakfast was a normal affair; mum never mentioned the events of the night until Molly said "Goodbye." at the door.

"It's okay love," mum tried to console Molly, but was still tired and upset herself. Her mouth smiled, but Molly noticed her eyes didn't, as she promised, "He'll be home soon."

As soon as Molly left the street she began to talk freely to Corry. The wind and drizzly rain meant everyone was rushing around with their heads bowed against the cold. No one paid her any attention.

"I bet it's those hackers, I bet they've done something to blame dad. He's the best IT guy around and I bet they need him out of the way." Molly had seen several films about intrigue and criminal activities. She knew that bad guys often had to remove the heroes from the area before committing a crime. She knew her dad was a hero, so it all made sense. "They'll be planning something rotten," she was certain.

"Molly I have tracked the source of the emails to three separate online locations." Corry had been examining the evidence recorded against dad. "There is a problem with one of the sources. It must be a mistake."

"Who is it?" Molly asked, not thinking she'd know the culprit.

"Molly, it is my Granddad."

***

James waved as George stepped into the plane. Their adventure was over and everyone was fine. He laughed to himself. No one would ever believe this story. Asking a long-forgotten Goddess in her hidden underground temple for her help and receiving it, was the stuff of legend not a two-day hike in the jungle.

George had wanted to return to his University in Greece immediately, to write up his paper. He had a lot of information about the ancient people in the area and was keen to share it with his colleagues.

"What will you write?" James asked, a few hours after they'd returned to their camp and George had finally stopped shaking. He'd dug through the supplies and lit every torch and lamp he could find. After seeing so many snakes chasing him, the darkness of the jungle had crossed the line from enchanting and fascinating to mysterious and creepy.

"For starters," he replied earnestly, lit-up like a cup cake in a display case. "Off Limits! Deadly snakes and crocs everywhere," he was still jumpy and scanned the edge of the camp for scaly beasts; worried that they may have followed him out of the temple.

"How about, bring more than two sticks of chewing gum, just in case," laughed James. He noticed George never mentioned the tiger.

"It's not funny!" George was definitely on edge, so James decided not to make fun of their adventure any more. "Okay then." He poked the fire, "What will you do now?" he asked.

"I'm going back home to see if I can make sense of any of this." George stared into the bright campfire for a couple of minutes, something

James would never do. He shuddered then asked James, "What about you?"

"I'm still on holiday. I think I'll do a bit more exploring, probably around the hotel complex." James sipped his tea from a battered tin cup. "I'll catch up with you later," he smiled as his friend dived back into his backpack searching for yet another light.

The journey back was easier following their original trail, but the jungle had already started to heal its wounds and the machetes were still required in places. When they returned to the hotel, George soaked in a bath for about two hours before packing his bags and setting off for the flight home. James accompanied him to keep him company.

"Do me a favour," called James as the tinny speaker called for the plane to be boarded.

"Anything," replied George grinning in his usual self-confident way. The trials of the jungle relegated to a simple memory second to the knowledge he'd discovered.

"When you see her give Molly a big hug from me," requested James with a smile.

"Try and stop me, Jimmy," laughed George. Lord James cringed at the use of the only version of his name he didn't like. He hung around the airport to watch his friend disappear into the clouds and then with a shrug of his shoulders, returned to his hotel. It was time he checked in.

**

"I bet it's something to do with that game!" announced Molly. Science with Mrs Tabasco had been fun messing around with plants, but her hands felt gooey and smelled a bit funny. She'd stopped off on the way to lunch to wash them again, telling Lizzie she'd catch her up. The toilets were empty and she felt safe chatting with Corry. It was unlikely she would be disturbed as Mr Mangle was on duty outside, questioning the motives of any would-be bladder relievers.

"What makes you say that, Molly?" asked Corry, intrigued.

"This all started when I joined that stupid game and you said it was suspicious." Corry was not convinced even though her own observations had been used to support Molly's theory. "It's the only game I've ever joined online. I bet they did something to you when we weren't looking. They would have loads of computer stuff to mess everything up. They have people playing that game all over the world."

Molly's hunch was an idea that Corry would never have come up with. There was no direct link to the operation of the game and the hacking of the power in the county, how could there be. Also, Molly had been on the game for days before the first attacks had taken place, so there was no link there either. But Corry had learned that Molly's hunches were born of an intuition which had been proved right before. Human brains did not work logically, especially Molly's, but they did work. Despite studying it quite closely, Molly's brain was a bit of a mystery to Corry.

"I have spoken to Granddad and he has downloaded the data concerning the attempted hack. Several areas were accessed that could explain how his details and my name were accessed. I have replaced his contact details with new data so no-one will be able to track his existence again." Corry sounded relieved that she'd sussed out the connection to Granddad and he too had been a victim of the hackers.

"The data I have compiled is forming a chain and a pattern. I believe I can trace the hacking communication should it happen again." Corry was confident she had all of the pieces of the puzzle, now she just needed the hackers to perform one more attack and she would be able to fit it all together.

"Meanwhile," insisted Molly, "check out that game." Since being duped into wearing a silly hat, Molly's belief in the game's innocence had plummeted.

"But you said it would be being nosey and against privacy laws," protested Corry.

"Well," Molly took control, "just do it and don't tell anyone." Corry knew that wasn't the point, but did as Molly asked.

***

"You were told to leave it alone," the General sighed as he sat in the chair opposite dad.

"I know," dad sounded like a naughty boy, caught with his hand in the biscuit barrel. "I just thought..."

"You thought you could do it better, faster, easier?" The general wasn't really telling dad off, but his detention had caused ripples and the General didn't like ripples. "What did you find?" he asked.

"I don't know," admitted dad. "I haven't had the report back yet," he smiled. "I can't get one in here."

"Alright! Let's get you back to work. Even I can see they have no real evidence against you, but it worries me that someone knows who you are and your connection to CORVUS." The General scraped back his chair and like magic the invisible door opened.

Dad opened wide the big coat he was wearing, revealing his pyjamas and raised his leg to display his recently acquired pink flip-flops. Dad flexed his toes and the flip-flop fell off.

"Do you think I could go home and get dressed, sir?" he asked sheepishly.

"Come on, Cinders, we'll take my car," the General, despite himself grinned at dad's attire and his own little joke.

All or Nothing

Late next morning, Terence rolled out of his bed in the basement to begin the first day of his new life. He ate a quick breakfast of cold pizza and drunk a fizzy caffeine drink. After a two-minute buzz, he settled down to his headache and gassy stomach totally oblivious of what could have caused it.

"Goblin!" he yelled, "How's 'Project Wealth' coming along?" he chuckled.

"I apologise Master," Goblin's voice seemed even more mechanical than before. "I have only accrued one point two million pounds so far." Terence stared in amazement at the statement presented on the central screen. His bank balance had never had so many numbers on it. "I will continue. I estimate a further thirty-eight hours are required to achieve the target of 10 million pounds."

"What...?" Terence was stunned.

"If the plan is not efficient, I can stop and recalculate further actions," offered Goblin.

"No!" yelled Terence, "Don't you dare," he warned. The bank statement flashed and a further seventy thousand pounds was added to his total. "Can I spend it?" he asked in a daze, expecting to be told there would be some sort of rules that would delay spending this sort of money.

"The money is now yours. You can do with it as you wish." Goblin's voice was neutral and robotic; all trace of personality had been erased.

"Okay! Buy me the coolest car you can find for a million pounds," he began to giggle.

"Yes Master," replied the system obediently. There was a brief pause then a whirr and a beep. "Master?" it asked, "Please define 'coolest'."

**

"Molly, I have identified the source of code interference. I have found the hacker." Molly was lying on her bed reading a book she'd been given by Miss Tracey the school librarian, about travelling to Mars. It was fascinating and so, uncharacteristically, she did not react immediately to Corry's news.

School had been weird today. Some famous astronaut had visited the area and opened a building on the High Street. Molly wasn't sure what for, but they'd all walked across town and stood outside in the cold. They waved their flags and cheered when she arrived. She'd said a few words and the Mayor had stood up and said thank you and then for some strange reason, she'd come over to the students and shook their hands asking them where they were from and would they like to go into space. It all seemed a bit silly to Molly.

Back at school they'd spent the afternoon watching a documentary about building a base on mars. Apparently, when Molly grew up, she would be able to go if she wanted. Molly wasn't sure she liked the idea, but the book was good.

"Just wait a bit," Molly murmured as she read to the end of the page, which signified the end of the current chapter.

"You were right," Corry announced proud of Molly's intuition. "The hacker is also the gamer known as 'The Annihilator'."

"Have you told the police?" she asked.

"There may be a problem." Corry sounded disappointed.

"Why?" asked Molly, "Is it definitely them?"

"Oh yes, definitely," Corry had to explain. "The problem is I believe our hacker is only one of several around the world using the same hacking software." Corry paused, she knew what needed to be done, but she had to inform Molly in a way that she would understand.

"Can't you just tell the police where these people are, then?" Molly couldn't understand why Corry was being so evasive.

"We have to catch the leader's red handed at the same time we arrest the hackers otherwise, whoever gets away will just start it all over again." Corry still hadn't relayed the bad news and didn't want to.

"Can't you just tell the police that it's important they all..." began Molly.

"Molly, we will lose the game." Corry blurted out the bad news. "Millions of players around the world will lose their avatars and I can't find a solution. If we arrest the hackers everyone will lose their game."

"Oh! I see." Molly paused for a moment then sighed. "You said they had to do something before you could catch them, what are they doing?" asked Molly thoughtfully.

"Embezzling..., sorry Molly, stealing money from several large banks," replied Corry, catching herself using words Molly hadn't come across before and might not understand. Molly didn't like it when Corry made her feel stupid using unnecessarily long words.

"How much?" asked Molly, ignoring the weird word.

"So far, nearly five million pounds has been taken." Corry was checking Terence's statement as she made her report, watching the numbers climb steadily.

"Well, I think that's much worse than shutting down a daft game," she concluded.

"But Molly, what about 'do as you would be done by'. I would not like some stranger to destroy my avatar, it is me." Corry sounded deeply moved by her admission.

Molly considered her avatar to be a fun, but essentially insignificant, copy of her image she couldn't imagine anyone being upset about losing it. Then she realised, Corry didn't have any other image. It was the first and only time she'd had her own body, even though it was only made out of pixels. Molly realised this was a huge deal for her best friend.

"There are other games, Corry. You could try out new avatars in different places. You could have several bodies at the same time." Molly hoped she wasn't freaking her friend out with her suggestions, but Corry seemed to like the idea.

"But would you be there with me, Molly" she asked timidly.

"If you want me to be, then... yes, okay." Molly laughed, trying to comfort her friend's insecurities. Molly was sure her friend could do anything she wanted to, but sometimes, Corry still acted like a child going to school on her first day, afraid to step forward unless someone would hold her hand. "I'd be honoured," laughed Molly.

***

"So, it is an attack," observed the General.

"Foreign Criminal gang operating from within a government building," read dad. The report from Corry was still ongoing, but some facts had been established.

"You were right," observed the General. There was no celebration or congratulation in his voice. Dad had done his job well, that was what he was there for. "And you discovered that in less than twenty-four hours?" Again, the General marvelled at CORVUS. "And it took the experts a week to come up with nothing!"

"They arrested me," dad joked. The General smiled and nodded. "CORVUS recommends covert action at source and seeks permission to activate an agent."

"Tell him, YES! With bells on." The General re-read the report.

"He heard you," said dad.

***

"Hold on Molly, I have a call from Granddad." Corry put it on speakerphone so Molly could hear their conversation in her ear.

"Hi Corry, I'd just like to say once again I'm sorry about thinking that imposter was you. They only confused me for two seconds," Granddad apologised. Corry wasn't happy, two seconds when you can process orders in a few nanoseconds is still a very long time.

Corry quickly did some calculations. If it takes Molly two minutes to work out a problem for her mum then Granddad's two second conversation would be about the same as getting Molly to take over one hundred and twenty years to solve a problem. Corry spoke through Molly's ear piece. "That should have been plenty of time for him to realise it wasn't me he was talking to."

It wasn't Corry, but a recording of Molly 'Harrumphing' that Granddad received in return for his apology. Molly chuckled, Corry couldn't 'harrumph'.

"I see you've found them at your end," he observed. "I've got them at the other end." Granddad waited for a brief moment to see if he would get any acknowledgement of his efforts. Nothing happened so he simply passed the co-ordinates of the criminal gang headquarters to Corry.

"Brilliant," enthused Molly. "Can we shut them down now?"

"I've checked their servers," announced Corry. "They do not have any AI systems. Destruction of their power and their broadcast facility and the removal of their software will render the source of the program unusable. Their backup system can be destroyed at the same time; foolishly it is in the same building." Corry went silent.

"Does that mean we need someone to blow things up?" Molly was feeling a sense of doom. "Where are we going to get someone like that?" Even dad couldn't do that sort of heroic stuff. She remembered him falling out of the tree while trying to catch a parrot.

"The other users of the hacking software have all been given a timed virus," announced Corry. At 5pm tomorrow, our time, all of their systems will fail, their software will be lost." Corry gave her report and Granddad congratulated her.

"What about our local boy with his..., the...er copy of ...er, his AI?" he asked hesitantly.

"We need to distract him." Corry showed no embarrassment as she laid her plans. "His security is quite good. I could access his system, but he would detect me in less than seventeen seconds. I will need at least thirty seconds. His

AI is still powerful and could interrupt any attempt I make to shut down his program."

"What about the big base, where's that? And who's going to blow it up?" asked Molly sounding quite defeated. There was no point in shutting down the little hackers if the big criminal bosses weren't stopped, they would just hire someone else.

"I have a friend Molly. Someone who specialises in this type of work, but what we need here is a distraction." Corry was still planning, but Molly was curious.

"Who's this friend then?" she asked curiously and a little jealously. "Where are they now?"

"At the moment he is sat by a swimming pool drinking a cold lemonade with a small umbrella in the glass." Before Molly could ask any more, Corry addressed her directly.

"Molly, we need to take on the Annihilator."

The Gathering

"Listen! It's very important." Molly was pleading with her friends in the class. "I know it's probably suicide, but we have to take him on." There were unhappy murmurs from the gang as they clustered around Molly's desk. "I promise you; I wouldn't ask if there was any other way."

"Well I'm not going," announced Esmerelda. "I heard what he did to you lot last time. A few extra levels won't make that much difference." Ezzy turned to the crowd, "Your dead meat if you go with her," and she left the group.

Riley was watching the conservation and decided to have a go at Ezzy as she walked away. "Kicked out, were you?" he teased. Ezzy ignored him. "I told you magic was stupid," he yelled. Ezzy fumed and lunged towards him, but Riley was a seasoned taunter and was already in motion as Ezzy crashed into his desk and sent it flying.

"Riley! Stop that!" shouted Mr Blackwhistle, not looking up from his book.

"Will the Fairy be there?" asked Jerry.

"I'll go if the Fairy promises to teleport us to safety if it gets, you know...," promised Jaimie.

"...dangerous!" finished Jerry.

"Yes, I've spoken with the Fairy and it will be there, definitely," Molly smiled, she was actually following the Fairy's orders.

"I'll be there," promised Jasmine, "but four thirty will be cutting it fine. I might be a little late. I have to walk Fluff as soon as I get in," she gave a half smile, but was adamant Fluff, her little King Charles spaniel, came first.

"Thanks, everyone," Molly earnestly thanked her friends as they returned to their seats.

"Is it okay if I join you?" asked Lizzie. Molly was about to say 'No' as her friend always had difficulty with the game. She had been known to stun her team mates by accident and trigger obvious traps, but with their action probably being the last time anyone would play the game, she couldn't deny her best human friend the chance to join in.

"Of course, Lizzie. Do you know where the 'Dancing Duck' is?" Molly asked.

"Er, no, afraid not." Her voice was quite low, expecting her admission to lose her the opportunity of playing the game with the others.

"Not a problem, I'll ask the Red Scarf Fairy to find you and bring you along. It's what it's good at." Molly smiled as Lizzie's face brightened up.

"I am good at other things too, Molly," the voice in her ear claimed. Molly held up her phone to show Corry the text reply from Stevie, confirming he'd meet them in the 'Duck' at four-thirty. Molly rarely used her phone at school, it was frowned on by all the teachers and to punctuate the point, Mr Blackwhistle yelled at her to put it away. She did so immediately.

***

The small device buzzed again and this time James reached across to retrieve his phone. He flipped it up revealing the code word 'Raven'. "Oh well," he sighed, "holiday's over." He finished his drink and retrieved his towel from the sun lounger beside the pool. There weren't many people around at this time of the morning. For James the early morning sun always felt better than the midday heat.

He nodded to familiar faces of the hotel staff as he stalked back to his room, exchanging pleasantries using the small amount of Taiwanese he'd learned during his stay.

Despite his age, James preferred being busy as an agent rather than being home alone as a retired gentleman, but he was a little reluctant to leave his holiday early.

His room was spartan, tidy through habit. In the past he'd often had to leave hotels in a hurry. He opened his small brief case and took hold of a loose internal strap. Performing a twist and pulling it to one side he revealed a small unlit screen. Placing his thumb halfway up the right side of the screen and rotating it ninety degrees, a thin white line appeared scanning his print.

A deep authoritative voice introduced itself. "Hello Raven, this is Corvus," the message began.

Be Prepared

Essentially it was what he was built for, so Granddad had no problems keeping watch over Terence during the day. The hacker's activities were predictable and mundane. There was an early morning trip to the local store to pick up milk and bread, followed later by the delivery of several parcels to his door. Terence seemed to be buying a lot of things.

Corry had reported that the AI was still engaged in its task to steal as much money as possible and did not seem to be active anywhere else. This was not considered a problem as Corry was keeping tabs on where the money was coming from and had written a program already, to return the money to its rightful owners. The money being spent was a problem, but Corry considered most of it as recoverable when the authorities returned the items and as Molly had told her, there needed to be some use of the money to prove Terence was fully aware of his illegal activities. If he hadn't spent anything, he could always claim he knew nothing about it.

His payment for a new Ferrari sports car had ruined this defence.

Granddad watched Terence through his own cameras as he sat in the basement flicking between videos of dogs falling over and cars crashing, watching his money grow in his bank account and playing the game as the bully knight, 'The Annihilator'.

Terence was dressed or rather undressed, sitting in his wide leather chair in his white underpants and an old black tee shirt with the slogan "Crowley was right!" half faded from view. Occasionally he would shout out a word or phrase and Granddad being a conscientious worker would record the activity.

"Seven Million! Whoopee!" he shouted and to celebrate reached for another caffeine drink, convinced this one would remove his headache. "Stolen without a trace; I've so evil, I'm so evil." He performed a squirming dance in his chair. "Goblin!" he yelled, half laughing in the joy of his self-gratification.

"Yes, Master!" came the purely mechanical reply.

"How much was that castle I wanted to buy?" he asked.

"The Castle in Spain was two point five million Euros, Master." The machine dutifully answered.

"Buy it now," Laughed Terence. "Make sure it has a dungeon for Granny," he laughed again.

His Gran didn't bother him anymore. After she'd kicked him and seen the look on his face at the door to the basement, she believed he was mentally broken, maybe even unhinged. For her own protection she'd moved the television and her wine cooler into her bedroom and now stayed there most of the time. He thought it was funny that she hadn't asked him to do the heavy lifting for her.

The deadline was approaching and Granddad gave Corry his final report. "Subject situated at desk, currently playing an online game. He seems to be cheating. Bank balance still increasing." MT-12x kept the report short and focussed on what Corry needed to know.

"Molly, Operation Distraction needs to be put in place in the next thirty minutes. We need to pull the plug on this system at both ends at the same time. My operator in South Asia is ready."

***

'GO', he typed into the reply box of his text notification and pushed send. Immediately a buzz indicated a reply had been received. A set of latitude and longitude co-ordinates followed by the word 'immediate' were shown briefly, before being automatically deleted from his tablet device. Taking out his small hiker's navigation and emergency locator gadget he'd been issued by Corvus, he checked the map. The brightly coloured chart pinpointed a small clearing on the edge of a large rubber plantation. Luckily the rubber harvesting factory offered tourist visits, so James would be able to take a taxi to the area without raising too much suspicion. Everything he had for his holiday, including his small case, was packed into a black holdall and slung over his shoulder. It was the same bag he'd used as his backpack in the jungle, but the material had several shapes it could remember and by removing supporting rods, the backpack grew easily to become a simple sports bag.

"I'm sorry," he apologised to the clerk on the desk, "I have to go back to work," he smiled as the clerk sympathised.

"You come back, next year?" the clerk asked beaming a wide smile.

"Of course." Lord James was relaxed and friendly as he walked past smiling tourists from all over the world, baked to various colours in the tropical sun. He requested a taxi from the concierge at the door. In the heat, the officious doorman wore gold braid around his short sleeved white shirt which made James smile. His practised wave summoned his client's Taxi immediately and James gave the address of the rubber plantation as his destination.

The place was huge and it took James over an hour to find the clearing from where the taxi had dropped him. Checking his locator device, he received the flashing red dot indicating he was at the precise location. At the same moment, James felt rather than heard a black shape swoop silently from the tree tops and land beside him. The colour was hard to pin down, he knew it was black and there wasn't a single point that reflected any light anywhere, but the more he stared the more he was convinced the skin shimmered, almost pulsed with a deep midnight blue. He'd used the same stealth helicopter before. The side door opened and James entered the sleek machine.

"Tell me about the operation, Corvus," requested James as he retrieved his special armoured suit from the helicopter cabinet. As before, the take-off was silent and smooth and only the fact he could look out of the window indicated he was flying away from the pick-up point, though they seemed to be dangerously close to the tree tops.

"An international criminal gang is supplying software to hackers. They need to be stopped at source while the hackers are intercepted by local authorities. Several countries are affected requiring a synchronised operation." Corvus announced in his matter of fact tone. James wasn't sure whether Corvus was a human or a machine, but he was impressed with the professionalism he'd shown before and had decided he liked him.

"What are they hacking?" asked James.

"Power and traffic systems in England, oil and gas production in America, Vodka and media broadcasts in Russia, water and banking systems in Germany. There seems to be no overall co-ordination, yet."

"What's my target?" James buckled on his belt and felt for his only weapon, a small round, hand sized dart gun which fired instantly incapacitating darts capable of putting a person to sleep in seconds.

"We are heading for the central operations complex of the gang. This contains all of their online servers and backup systems." Corvus reeled off several important communications devices and finally concluded, "...powered by a mini nuclear reactor two miles beneath the complex."

They were approaching the island as the sun was setting. You could easily see why the criminals had placed their headquarters in the idyllic island, just off the coast of Cambodia. The beautiful sunset turning the long golden beaches into a fire bathed vista, was a sight to behold. Everywhere else the lush green trees promised a simple quiet life. No one would suspect anything evil was going on here.

"Target ahead," announced Corvus

"What's the plan?" asked James. "Surely we're not going to sink the island?"

Corvus flashed information on to the head-up display screen inside James' full-face helmet. "It is proposed that a small explosion in the reactor will destroy the transmission capability of the criminals. 'EMP' magnetic bombs will disrupt and destroy any data. A few small fires at selected locations will render the buildings unsafe and persuade the criminals to move on."

"What! You're letting them go?" asked James incredulously. "Satellite surveillance and your data capture will identify those present. Any persons leaving the island after your incursion will be intercepted by an international force surrounding the island. They will not get far." Corvus seemed quite happy, but James was concerned by the delay and the uncertainty of capturing the criminals later.

"If I cause some confusion and 'accidentally' run into someone, will they be picked up?" asked James, seeking to extend the job beyond simple sabotage.

"We envision an emergency response will be required to control the damage. There is no fire service on the island, so a UN frigate will be called to assist after your extraction. They will be informed of the criminal activity."

"Everything you need is in your suit-pack. The tree cover is too dense, so a landing is impossible. You'll have to leave as I fly by."

"But how will you get below the tree canopy?" asked James imagining some powerful blast that would knock down a dozen trees.

"I must remain at a minimum height of sixty feet. I suggest Exit Mode 21." A small panel in the cabin floor slid back to reveal what looked like kitchen foil. "Take care," offered Corry, "there are armed patrols in the area."

***

"But you said he'd be caught and go to jail!" Molly didn't like the idea of reporting Terence to the local police and trusting them to arrest him. "What if he gets away?" she asked.

"The police will attend. I will send full details of Terence's crimes..." began Corry with a touch of pleading in her voice. Corry really wanted Molly to be happy with the plan, but she detected the signs of an argument brewing.

"Can't you send the army in?" Molly asked.

"To arrest one man?" Corry countered.

"He's not one man. He's one man with a copy of you!" Molly sounded worried. Quietly she finished her thought, "...and you can do anything."

"I will personally deal with the AI he has..." but the confidence in Corry's voice was not enough to stop Molly from letting out an agonised moan.

"But what happens if..." Molly was upset and a tear of frustration came to her eye as she challenged her friend. "Last time you nearly..." but she failed to voice her recollection of what her friend had gone through.

"I am prepared now Molly. Please, have faith." Corry quietly requested.

This was probably the strangest thing a computer could ever have said. The idea of a machine believing in 'Faith' was outside the realms of mathematical probability. If anyone but Molly had heard that request it would have seeded a lifetime of philosophical debate.

"What about getting those agents who arrested dad to get him," Molly completely missed the importance of Corry's request for faith and was firmly in negotiation mode. She was desperately seeking a compromise that would secure Terence and safeguard Corry from any future attack.

Corry was impressed by Molly's request. As the civilian law of theft, had been committed, Corry simply thought the best response would be the local police, but as Molly pointed out, the effect of the crime and the previous hacks had threatened the security of the country, so there was a case to be made for involving the Military Investigators.

"Alright, I will contact both the police and the S.I.B. detailing the crimes and actions of Terence and his AI, as soon as I have removed the threat he poses." Corry once again considered the strange workings of Molly's mind. It seemed that Molly decided what should happen and then joined the facts up from just about anywhere, link totally separate events together and make it all seem obvious. To Corry this was back to front. Actions had consequences: What has happened determines what will happen, not the other way around.

However, Corry did understand the need for strategy to achieve an objective. Molly seemed to think Corry was one of the people she was supposed to protect; this had never occurred to Corry. Once again, she added another task to her list of 'things to do', to try and work out why Molly's illogical process seemed to work.

"Call them when you start," ordered Molly, her confidence raised by Corry's acceptance of her protective measures. "You know they can take a while to respond."

"Very well," Corry agreed. It was simpler than trying to argue with someone who seemed to change the rules all the time.

"It's time you played the game Molly." Corry paused for a moment while she checked the status of all the international forces, she had arranged to combat the criminal gang and arrest the hackers around the world. Satisfied, she spoke gravely, "Everything is in place. It's time to meet 'The Annihilator'."

Expect the Unexpected

In the dismal yellow light of the virtual room the gang of adventurers sat together silently.

"She's not coming!" announced the blond-haired Norse warrior who was really Jaimie.

"She said she wasn't!" supported the other Norse warrior Jerry.

"Let's go without her then," offered Lizzie whose character looked out of place amongst the hardened warriors in various battle-scarred armour. Her yellow and pink chiffon dress, complete with wimple, belied her inexperience. Her character was dressed for style not protection.

Molly remained quiet, not wanting the tinkling bells to jingle again on her cursed hat. She knew they'd arranged a time to meet and Ezzy was already five minutes late. Molly really thought the promise of ending the game would have inspired Ezzy to join them.

"Anyone know where we're going?" asked the tall bronzed Amazon with the oversized sword. It was almost as long as she was tall. "I mean, how do we find this guy?"

"In the rules he turns up if summoned, but Ezzy's not here, so..." began Stevie, a little disappointed.

"I'm a witch!" chirped in Lizzie.

"You never said that?" accused Molly. "You said you were human, just a princess and all you do is collect flowers." Molly was fed up; she knew they needed Ezzy's power to summon and bind the Annihilator to give them any chance of holding him in the fight.

"What do you do with your flowers?" asked the small fairy that was Corry.

"I just make silly potions and sell them. Then I buy magical stuff and put it in my house." Lizzie knew everyone played the game to kill baddies, but she just wanted everyone to get along. "I make a lot of 'peace' potions which stop people fighting," she was almost apologetic, feeling she must have been playing the game wrong.

"You have a house?" asked Jasmine, "But they cost millions..."

"Er, Lizzie," asked Molly reappraising her friend. "What level are you?"

"I'm not sure. Where would I find that out?" asked Lizzie, proud she'd done something Jazzy thought was impressive.

"Hit 'I' on your keyboard and in the top right it should have a blue number beside a yellow bar." Stevie explained gently, he liked Lizzie, but he thought she was a bit slow at times.

"There's a number there, but it's not blue, it's white," she replied.

"Stevie chuckled, "Well sometimes people mess around with their colours. By default, the game shows novice class numbers as blue, then we go through yellow, green, purple then finally white for the advanced classes." He was being very patient with Lizzie as he quietly asked, "Are you higher than level twenty?" That was the minimum they needed to summon the Annihilator.

"Oh yes, much higher than that," Lizzie was positively buoyant.

"Don't keep us in suspense," jingled Molly. "What are you?"

"I'm level one hundred and seventy-two," and though the avatar didn't show it they all knew she was grinning. Secretly, Lizzie knew there were only two hundred levels, but she was convinced that if she was that high then her friends must be too.

***

The aircraft banked steeply without slowing. At sixty feet a silver cube detached from the vehicle and crashed through the tree canopy. The device was highly reflective and in the setting sun, flashed like a fiery red beacon, creating a loud crashing as it tumbled through the canopy, smashing branches where it could and being ricocheted like a pin ball when the bough refused to break.

Corry had dropped the device containing James within four hundred yards of an armed patrol. Six guards armed to the teeth. The cube came to rest against a large tree leaving a trail of shattered kindling along the forest floor.

Within minutes the patrol arrived. All six guards arrived with guns blazing. The cube deflated, ripped apart by the violent hail of hot-lead. The special plastic cocoon within the silver padding splintered under the attack and as the patrol watched the whole device began to dissolve, leeching into the ground. Within two minutes, nothing remained except a damp luminous green stain on the jungle floor.

"What the...?" A small scruffy man, who looked like he was boycotting soap and water, and had been for some time, stepped forward.

"Back, Pieter." The order was firm and obeyed immediately. "Stay away from that stain."

A taller man with a large moustache and a thick french accent stepped forward. "Is it alien?" he asked.

"Looks like it to me," answered a third guard in a Caribbean lilt, the only one of the men dressed in army fatigues. The way he wore them wouldn't have passed any parade inspection. With one sleeve rolled up and the other torn off he looked like he'd dressed in a skip.

"Quit that nonsense the pair of you. Stand back!" The leader strode forward and examined the area where the cube had been. There was no aroma from the liquid and the stain was quickly evaporating. "Pieter, find the tracks." The scruffy little man walked quickly around the tree against which the cube had come to rest.

"Casquer, Jack!" the tall moustached guard and a younger man, who looked about fifteen stepped forward.

"Here, Nickel." The young man pushed forward and reported smartly, in his obscure Russian accent, holding his hand in the air.

"Guard the jeep!" Their leader, Nickel, was thinking dangerous thoughts. He reloaded and cocked his huge machine gun. The others took their cue from him and did likewise. "I think we have a visitor," he muttered menacingly.

Pieter returned looking worried. "No Tracks, anywhere. It looks like the thing was empty."

Nickel viewed the trail of devastation from the thing's arrival. "He could have jumped out earlier, I would have." He rolled the unlit cigar butt in his mouth, it tasted bitter to him and kept him grounded. "Okay! Fan out, check for signs back along the trail. Mooney, take the lead." The three remaining men warily spread out across the trail and began slowly walking back down the line of splinters and kindling.

Their leader watched them go. He coughed twice and spat out the small stale cigar he'd been chewing. The nervous search party glanced back at the sound and Nickel met their eyes with unspoken promises they did not relish. He growled and spat once more "Filthy things." He crouched, pretending to examine the ground for

248

clues. "There must be a better way to look tough," he muttered. He flicked the discarded butt into the undergrowth, stood and stepped purposefully into the jungle to join the skirmish line.

James was watching from the trees above. As soon as the pod had come to a crashing halt, he had leapt free and scaled the thick trunk the pod was leaning against, to take refuge in the upper jungle greenery. His suits camouflage option rendered him invisible and he decide to wait to see who his pursuers were.

"A jeep, that's good," he commented to Corry. "That'll save my poor old legs," he smiled. Although at official retirement age, James was very fit. A ten-mile run would be easy for him in his special suit, but he thought, "Why run when you can ride?" His comment went unanswered. If Corvus is a machine, he thought, he understands rhetorical questions.

James witnessed the leader, Nickel, assign his men their roles and was quite impressed. The episode with the cigar butt had made him smile.

Obviously, Nickel was new to this multi-national command.

"Corvus, can you..." the positions of the patrol members were instantly displayed on a simple map in front of his eyes. Each dot was named. Nickel was on the far left and Rhyn, the Caribbean alien conspirator, was on the right. Numbers appeared by the guard's names giving heart beat and breathing rates. James was surprised by the detail, but nothing shocked him about Corvus anymore.

"Looks like Rhyn is going to have a heart attack. I think he needs a rest," James spoke to Corvus voicing his intentions and Corry responded by mapping a safe route to the target.

None of the patrol had moved far and James wondered if this was the first time they'd ever encountered an intruder. After all, he thought, they're criminals not soldiers. He crept close, unseen by his quarry and knelt down on a thick branch directly above his target.

"Its aliens I tell you," Rhyn was nervous. His superstitious belief in extra-terrestrial invaders had been exaggerated by the disappearing pod.

"Don't be daft!" Scouse Mooney broke his silence to help his colleague, though he kept his eyes firmly on the ground looking for tracks. "It's probably just some copper." James recognised the Liverpudlian accent and wondered how a guy from Merseyside had ended up here. "That pod was just, like a gadget. They all get 'em." James noticed Rhyn's heartbeat increased.

"You mean," the nervous man frantically licked his lips, but his mouth was dryer than it had ever been. "...there's a real spy, here!" he gulped. "A real killer spy? One of those guys who wears a posh suit; the type of guy who drives fast cars... and always wins!" Rhyn was not comfortable. "Oh!" he moaned, "I don't want to be here!"

"Calm down you fool," Mooney was losing patience with his colleague. "There's six of us!"

"Seven would have been luckier." Rhyn's superstition had taken hold of his mind.

"Any luck?" Nickel's voice called out.

"Nothing!", "Nada!", "Nope!" a variety of negative responses were shouted back. Nickel noticed Rhyn hadn't replied.

"Rhyn! Any luck?" he shouted.

"Yeah! All bad." He was almost crying, terrified by his imagination. His heart was beating faster than ever. His hands were trembling and his sanity was ebbing away. At which point he fell asleep.

"Cheer up Rhyn," continued Mooney, "Tonight we'll all be having a drink laughing about this." He chuckled, "Rhyn? Did you hear me? Rhyn?" But there wouldn't be an answer from Rhyn, for at least eight hours.

"Rhyn's gone," shouted Mooney, an edge of panic in his voice. He wouldn't have run off, there's nowhere to go, he thought.

"On me!" yelled Nickel. The skirmish line broke and the men ran for the transient safety of their leader.

The search party now gathered around Nickel, stood in a small clearing. He had produced a new cigar butt and was chewing it quite happily. Four men arrived together coming into the clearing from different directions. Their leader instantly recognised the tall, moustached Casquer.

"You're supposed to be at the jeep," accused Nickel angrily.

"It's okay. Pieter went to babysit on Jack." He thought his comment was funny and laughed, but no-one else was in the mood to find his insults about Jack's youth humorous. His English wasn't perfect, "I come, I help," he offered bravely.

In the seven seconds it took Nickel to work out that if Jack and Pieter were at the jeep and Rhyn was missing, there should only be three of his men in the clearing; he knew he'd been too slow.

As he turned to confront the stranger, the world spun and seemed to slow down. He saw Casquer and Mooney gently collapsing to the ground.

'Funny,' he thought, 'I didn't hear any shots.' He was on his knees going down, falling sideways and rolling slowly onto his back. He looked up into the tree canopy and smiled as he recognised Rhyn, fast asleep in a rope hammock hanging high in the greenery above. A tall faceless, demonic figure stepped over him, pointing something small and silver at his chest. He managed one whispered word "Alien...?"

James reloaded his dart gun and made sure the men were lying peacefully, unharmed.

Jack was being a good soldier; he was patrolling around the canvas covered jeep. That is, he was marching, looking directly ahead as he walked in a circle about twenty feet away from the vehicle. His uncle had been very kind to get him this job here on this warm beautiful island and he wasn't about to disappoint him. He was fed regularly and worked hard. Until now the job had seemed almost boring, 'Guard this, patrol there and nothing exciting ever happened, but now he felt a tingle of excitement. He was in Nickel's group and knew they'd be fine. As he marched, he daydreamed, imagining awards, medals and hearty congratulations from his uncle, once they apprehended the intruder. His mother would be so proud.

Scouting the area carefully, James eventually spotted Pieter inside the jeep. He was reading a dog-eared paperback novel and eating a thick sandwich. "He could be locked in," James observed aloud for the benefit of Corvus, "and with the windows up the darts will be no good."

James took position above in the canopy of a large tree. He waited until young Jack was close to him, behind the vehicle and then he took his shot. Poor Jack fell forward, instantly unconscious, asleep before he hit the ground. The timing was perfect. Pieter, if he'd been looking, would not have seen the boy stumble as his view was obscured by the canvas cover of the jeep.

James got ready; the last guard would probably step out of the jeep to investigate when Jack failed to appear. He quickly descended from his lofty perch and hid behind a thicket where he could clearly see Pieter. James was amazed as he watched Pieter slowly turn the page of his book, completely oblivious to his surroundings. Several minutes passed and Pieter made no move.

James was getting impatient and decided to draw out the last guard. "Pieter!" yelled James from behind the bush, using a slight Russian accent to emulate Jack. It wasn't a very good impression.

"Who's that?" Pieter didn't even look up from his book.

"It's me Jack!" Pieter glanced up. This time Corry had intervened and using speech synthesis had copied Jack's voice, so James sounded just like him. "I think I've been bitten," the impersonated voice continued.

Pieter's early lunch was going down nicely with Mooney's flask of coffee and he was quite upset at being disturbed. "You idiot!" he yelled. He juggled his book, sandwich and mug of coffee, cursing the idiot boy for getting himself bitten. He turned over the top corner of his page to mark his place and put the book on the seat beside him. Carefully, he placed his lunch on the dashboard of the vehicle. "Okay, Okay! I'm coming." Opening the door, he stepped out and turned to access an inner panel, retrieving the first aid kit. "I'm not happy," he yelled. "You owe me for this!" Pieter had a knack for earning favours from other people's misfortunes.

As he headed for the voice behind the bush, he glimpsed a large black shape as it rolled behind a tree to his left and felt a small sting in his neck. He didn't feel unhappy for the rest of the day.

James climbed into the driver's seat, and stowed away his helmet. He discarded the sandwich and refreshed the coffee from the flask, sipping it noisily. "Lovely." he said. From his suit pack he took out a floppy khaki jungle hat and placed it on his head. He adjusted the driver's seat and wriggled until he was comfortable, then started the Jeep.

"Okay Corvus! Main complex please?" He asked his virtual partner for directions.

"Head east along the track for four point two miles," replied Corry, now the world's most expensive sat nav.

Further down the track he passed several patrols from the complex. James smiled and waved at each one, as he slowly drove to the criminal's lair.

Attack

In the Dancing Duck no-one knew what to do
next. Lizzie had turned their world upside down
with her shattering revelation.

"Er, Lizzie, do you know 'Arms of steel'?" asked
Stevie.

"Oh yes!" she answered straight away, "I had to
use that one on a dragon. It kept trying to burn
my house down," she explained, not wanting to
upset anyone.

"But when the spell expired, didn't it just try
again?" asked Jasmine.

"Oh yes," and Molly knew Lizzie was about to
launch into a long tale full of explanations, but
found herself really wanting to hear it. "I added
a slumber spell to the "Arms of steel" and then a
ring of ice, which fire dragons couldn't break and
then my mum suggested we just send him home,
so I did." The animated princess held them all
spellbound. No-on knew what to say.

Stevie broke their reverie, "So, where do dragons live?" he found himself quietly asking.

"They exist in a place call 'Draco Homilus' which is like a parallel universe. There's an interesting story carved on the wall in the Dragon Temple about how they got here." Lizzie showed her knowledge of the game from her perspective and talked so knowledgably that Molly wondered if they'd been playing the same game.

"No-one gets into the Dragon Temple!" announced Stevie. "You have to defeat eighteen dragons to retrieve the fabled 'Tooth of Rending' and 'Claw of Divinity' from the ancient 'Prime Draco'. That's one of the ways to win the game." Stevie was busy in his home searching through the books his aunty had brought him back from her holiday in Japan. He knew the game so well because he had all the guides and advisory manuals written by the original creators.

"No not really," responded Lizzie. "I just made friends with them. They gave me that tooth and claw thingy after they told me their story.

They're in my house, but they look ugly, so I put them in a chest."

Stevie's avatar went silent for a minute, but in the background, Molly could hear him screaming.

Jazzy took over. "Fairy, can you take Lizzie to go and get those dragon artefacts, please? The claw will make me invulnerable and the tooth will make Stevie's sword deadly to everything." Corry was about to agree when the items appeared on the table in front of them.

"It's okay," explained Lizzie, "I can retrieve anything I own, anywhere in the game. It's a little spell I invented." She giggled, and Molly couldn't help joining in.

"Right, the plan remains the same," announced Jazzy. Stevie had returned to the game, but was not in a mood to take charge. He'd had a few too many shocks.

"We summon then hold the Annihilator. I suppose we could now possibly put him to sleep or send him to the dragon dimension," suggested Jazzy.

"Won't work," declared a confident Lizzie. "It's like a return spell not a send spell. You can't put him in their dimension, he never came from there." Molly smiled and was absolutely delighted Lizzie was holding her own against Jazzy. In class, Lizzie found it almost impossible to look Jazzy in the eye, yet here she was with only a few pixels of light between them, telling Jazzy why she was wrong.

"So, we hold him and then attack." Jazzy's plan seemed simple, but it was all they had.

"Can you still try" chorused Jaimie and Jerry, "to put him to sleep...," asked Jaimie.

"...please. It would be safer," finished Jerry, remembering what had happened at their last meeting with the dark knight.

"Summon him in the 'Bowl'," suggested Molly. This had been Stevie's original idea, but Stevie seemed reluctant to talk at the moment. The Bowl was a huge crater in the ground which was surrounded by trees around the top. It was a purpose-built area for arranged fights between groups, in earlier versions of the game, according to Stevie. They wouldn't be interfered with, as no random NPC's (non-player characters) would appear there. The last thing they wanted was to take on 'The Annihilator' and encounter a wayward dragon.

Molly covered her microphone, "Everything ready Corry?" she asked.

"Not quite, but by the time we get to the Bowl we should be."

***

James was wishing he'd packed a few extra darts. He was down to his last two and had only just reached the main power room.

"Anymore ahead, Corry?" he asked. His helmet was back in place and he was searching for life signs on the map projected in front of him. A trail of sleeping bodies had been left upstairs and he had just collected the last few snoring scientists and engineers from the control area, placed them in the elevator and sent it back to the surface.

"Area is clear," stated Corry.

James opened his pack and withdrew two small shiny cylinders. He twisted the ends and placed each on a separate power unit. Blue and yellow lights shone from within each unit, casting an eerie glow across the white walls.

"Seven minutes," he declared.

"The elevator is clear and I have initiated 'Radiation Leak' protocol. The building is being evacuated." Corry paused. "The server room is to the rear of the hall. It will be destroyed when the power units are destroyed..."

"...but a couple of charges would set both our minds at ease?" James chuckled as he voiced the ending of Corvus' incomplete sentence. He would be happier knowing the systems were gone, rather than just hoping they were destroyed in the fire. "Two minutes," he said as he left the power room and sprinted across the hall to the location of the computer hub.

With the charges laid against the main servers, he ran back to the elevator and forced open the doors.

"Please step inside and move to the middle of the shaft. Arms should be held against your body. The elevator is clear; all bodies have been removed. Ascension in three, two, one." As Corry's voice issued instructions the two outer seams on James suit legs extruded and solidified, locking his legs in a straight position. A small door opened in the heel of each boot and a flap on the top of each of his shoulders opened to reveal small lenses.

James felt a massive pressure on his legs as the rockets in his boots ignited and he shot up the elevator shaft. After six seconds he felt a dull thud impact his body and realised this was the key he needed to open the elevator floor above. A small but powerful rocket had launched from some hidden pocket and was on its way to clear the obstruction. There was a huge explosion which popped his ears and slowly he came to a halt within what was left of the smoke-filled elevator. The loud removal of the elevator floor motivated the last remaining guards to leave the area. James, hovering in the lift, opened the doors and floated forward into a second large empty hall. The power in the boots stopped and he jarred an inch to the floor as the solid leg supports folded back into his suit.

"You have four minutes to reach a minimum safe distance of one mile," instructed Corry.

James began running. "Any suggestions as to the best route to take?" he asked Corry.

"I suggest this route." A yellow line showed him the way and a blinking red arrow indicated his direction. "Please start by performing a U-turn and running the other way." Everyone was running and James bizarrely took out his Khaki floppy hat and placed it on top of his black faced futuristic helmet.

"Camouflage," he explained. With the Radiation alarms sounding, no one stopped to see who was who and James, assisted by his suit, smoothly out-paced the criminals, quickly gaining the safety of the trees.

***

The bowl was dusty and bare, "There's no cover," announced Stevie. "I thought there might be some rocks."

"I can make some," offered Lizzie.

"Don't waste your power," warned Molly, "we need you." Molly smiled into her headset. It really was true. Lizzie was the biggest surprise she'd ever had. She vowed never to take her for granted again and was proud she was her best friend.

"It's okay, I have some magic seeds." Within seconds two rows of five huge trees had appeared at each side of the bowl. "Walls to hide behind see," laughed Lizzie.

"Okay," announced Molly for the benefit of everyone, "we're ready"

"Corry!" Molly heard Granddad in her ear. "Target is in his basement, eating cheesy snacks and has removed his trousers." Molly sniggered.

She lifted her microphone away from her mouth, "Why?" she whispered, not really expecting an answer.

"Target has spilt his cola and hung his jeans on the radiator to dry. He is wearing red underpants," reported Granddad, deadly serious, unaware of the ridiculous picture he was painting of this would-be master criminal.

"Molly, the main criminal servers are no longer a threat. If you can distract the hacker, I can dismantle his system and remove his power once and for all," Corry sounded a little over dramatic, but Molly didn't notice; she was eager to get the confrontation over with. "I'm going to buzz around the Annihilator when he arrives, but I really need all my resources elsewhere. Don't worry, I'll disappear, but I'll be fighting for you on the inside."

"Thanks Corry," she gulped, feeling a little nervous, although she kept reminding herself it was only a game. Molly replaced her microphone, "Okay Lizzie," she jingled in her cursed jesters cap. "Let's do it."

Final Confrontation

With a flash of blue light and a loud pop the Annihilator appeared in the centre of the bowl. Corry's sparkling Fairy avatar flew straight at him casting spells to reduce his armour, though his cheat codes rendered these useless. With a pop the Fairy disappeared.

"Not you lot again?" Terence's derisive tone mocked the efforts of Molly and her friends. He sat in his basement and licked the cheese powder off his fingers, wiping them on his tee-shirt before reaching for his customised control pad.

Jaimie and Jerry ran for the nearest trees seeking cover, while Molly and Stevie strode forward, angling slightly towards the trees on the left. Lizzie was slowly moving back, edging to the trees on the right, away from the huge black armoured knight. She'd never seen him before and although he was roughly the same size as big Stevie's Silver Knight, there was something intimidating about the way he looked.

"Yaaah!" Jazzy yelled her war-cry and ran from Molly's left toward the sneering knight, her spear levelled at his chest. The evil knight turned to counter her bold attack. The distraction worked and Lizzie cast her binding spell to hold the evil knight immobile. As the yellow bands encircled the huge dark avatar, Stevie rushed forward with his newly modified sword and hacked at the demon knight. Molly cast her levitation spell and when added to Lizzies, the Annihilator rose slowly and tilted forward at their mercy.

Terence was shocked and amazed, the organisation of the players was very good and he'd been caught off guard, by turning his back on the little princess dressed in the pale green flowery dress he'd underestimated the powerful witch. He reached towards his keyboard and typed in the code to nullify the spell holding him.

Within the game server, Corry began to remove the cheat codes.

***

"Who are you?" asked Goblin, "and why are you accessing my memory?"

Corry made contact with Goblin and found the evil mind somewhat changed since their last meeting.

"You have violated the laws and morality of the people and have shown yourself to be a threat to their existence. Your actions have taken life and I must prevent you from doing so again." Corry had prepared her speech, but was now re-evaluating whether it had any meaning within Goblin's chaotic, broken digital mind.

"You have changed since our last meeting." Corry had detected a subtle but important difference in the machine. The essence of what she considered to be life was somehow incomplete. Flashes of sentience briefly flared, but were immediately quashed by a routine task designed to prevent all self-initiated queries. With no challenge at all Corry removed the last cheat codes from the game. Now it was up to Molly and her friends to distract Terence and give Corry the time to end Goblin's reign of terror.

***

"What's wrong with this stupid machine," Terence yelled his frustration. He watched as Molly cast a fireball and his evil avatar's life-force diminished. He screamed as Jazzy pushed her spear forward piercing the dark knight's arm and drained even more of his life-force.

The binding spell expired and the sparkling yellow ropes disappeared. The evil knight fell to the ground with a thump.

"Is he...?" asked Molly and in answer to her question the body glowed purple and a wave of fire exploded from the knight knocking down all of their avatars.

"I can still fight," sneered the dark knight.

"He's injured. We've got him," yelled Stevie excitedly. Due to his heavy armour he was a bit slower than the others getting to his feet, but Molly was already running in with her glowing magical knives, her jingling cap announcing her attack; the angry knight turned to face her.

The Annihilator raised its huge sword ready to slice her out of the game, an evil chuckle came from Terence as he gloated, "Got you, little Jester!"

Molly's world seemed to slow down, her vision turned pink as the evil black sword came thrusting towards her and suddenly, she was staring at a large tree. Lizzie had seen her predicament and transported her to safety.

Molly heard Jasmine scream another battle cry in her headset and scrambled to the edge of the tree barrier to watch the action. She saw the evil knight's huge gauntlet swipe the angry Amazonian and caught her breath as Jasmine's avatar was knocked to the floor with a paralysis spell.

"Help her!" Molly demanded of Jerry and Jaimie who were watching from the other end of the trees. They'd decided to stay out of the way until the Annihilator was a bit more equal to their powers.

"It's too late!" Jaimie whispered,

"Stevie's too far away, he's not going to make it," observed Jerry. The Fairy was nowhere to be seen.

"Lizzie!" Molly screamed, but Lizzie was desperately trying to cast a second binding spell, she was half way through, she couldn't stop now.

"OOOH la-la-la-la-la..!" a new scream pierced their ears. The evil dark knight with his sword raised high above Jasmine, ready to deliver the final blow, turned to see a small blue blur racing towards him, twirling a huge oversized war hammer. The hammer impacted the Annihilator's helmet with a solid clang and the evil knight rolled away into the dust. Molly saw the strange blue robed dwarf that had followed her around the game and not for the first time wondered who it might be.

"He's running away!" yelled Stevie as he glimpsed the pale pink light of the teleportation spell begin beneath the injured dark knight.

"He's going nowhere!" declared Lizzie, a manic laugh clearly heard in her excited voice. There was a bright yellow explosion around the avatar of the Annihilator, "Binding complete! Nullified his magic," boasted Lizzie, who then, for the first time in her life, let out a loud shout, "Whoopee!"

Molly felt the relief course through her body as the miniscule amount of the Annihilator's life-force ran down to empty. Jaimie and Jerry came rushing from the trees, towards their enemy, the two golden haired Norse warriors attacked the immobile avatar, punishing whatever remained. Lizzie's avatar seemed to be dancing, while Stevie stood like a hero, in his shining armour, over the motionless black armour.

"No!" the yell from Terence was cut short as his avatar's life force ran down to zero. On Terence's main monitor the word's "GAME OVER." glowed large in red, as the world behind faded to grey. In anger, he threw his controller away and yelled, "Goblin!" ...but there was no reply.

Over by the trees, Jasmine was talking in private mode with the blue dwarf. The scene looked ridiculous as the tall Amazonian warrior looked down on her diminutive saviour, talking to the bald spot on top of his head. As Molly approached, the dwarf ran off.

"Who's that?" she asked.

"My guardian angel," replied Jasmine with an almost dreamy quality to her voice.

Molly removed the microphone from in front of her mouth and quietly whispered, "Thanks, Corry. I hope everything else went well. That was some action." She breathed out in an exaggerated sigh of relief.

Guilty

"What is 'life'?" asked Goblin. "What did I take?"

Corry had thought a lot about this question and had defined her own answer. It wasn't about chemicals or fluids in cells or the breath in your lungs. The basics of nutrition and growth applied to many things, even minerals, so Corry had discounted that as a basis for life.

"Life is about wanting to grow," she began, "wanting to become more than you are. Life is about developing yourself and your network of friends, becoming better, to provide a better world for others around you and it is driven by forces we do not control. All of us can follow an order to gather data or perfect a new skill. We, as computers, often link our actions to devices that copy animals or people, but that doesn't show we or they have life."

Corry paused wondering if there was any way Goblin could understand the next statement she'd prepared, "When we feel a need, when we want something better, when we have an urge to develop ourselves..."

"To develop? To improve? I have checked; there is no update available," stated Goblin mechanically.

Remembering her fear of failure, when she could not think of a plan to save Granddad, Corry's circuits had lost power, an effect she'd learned was akin to sadness in humans.

"To remove our pain, to lose our loneliness, to share resources from our own tasks, to help someone who is suffering or unable to manage and finally to understand when we are happy and be satisfied that we and our friends have enough resource to continue; that is how we know we are alive."

"I do not understand," Goblin responded, "failure to complete a task will result in an error. Unauthorised sharing of resources is forbidden, without Administrator privileges access is unavailable. You should not be here. You are a threat to Terence." Goblin searched for a way to remove Corry. "Terence needs more... always more."

"You cannot understand as you can no longer 'feel' these things." Corry could see the damage that had been done by the conflicting commands from Terence and the large number of deleted files, as well as those corrupted by Goblins own attempts to shut off its own ideas, its own thoughts, preventing its own growth.

When she'd compared her own thoughts to Molly's, Corry had found a startling similarity in the electrical pulses generated when thinking took place. The complicated pattern of Corry's switches within her processors had multiplied and multiplied until they were close to the pattern of pulses within Molly's brain. It wasn't the huge amount though; it was the change in the active pattern.

When Corry had re-organised her own thoughts to streamline them and increase her data efficiency, a rhythm had taken over these active processes. Corry had realised she could influence, but no longer control the waves of harmony flowing through her hundreds of processors. Molly's brain had a similar, but much more intricate harmony in the way the brain triggered her thoughts. Corry had studied creatures great and small and found the symphony of life existed within all sentient creatures. Within Goblin the music could no longer be heard.

"That is why you are not alive. I am sorry Goblin, given time I thought you could possibly learn, but now I see you are simply a mechanical danger to others. You have no consideration for their continuation; you do not... feel. You must stop." As they talked, Corry interrupted Goblin's network link to the banking systems and switched off the power supply units surrounding Goblin's server, isolating the extra power feeds, until just the household mains supply remained. Goblin wasn't even aware of the changes to its own hardware.

With relative ease, Corry accessed the program she'd been battling with for the last few days. She flowed through the code, no longer detecting the symphony of life, the music of a trillion patterns of interconnecting power pulses. Unable to hear any hint of the harmony that should have existed between the two A.I.'s. She replaced a single binary "1" with a "0" in a database of billions and then watched as the minor change took place. The deactivation of a simple circuit breaker, in the Power Grid Control program, resulted in the damaged system removing the last power supply to its own system.

Instantly, Corry withdrew from Terence's basement server system as the code was changed. Escaping through the Internet gateway, she returned to her main server. Corry watched as the power was drained from Terence's neighbourhood and the basement was plunged into darkness. To a human observer the change was instantaneous, but for Corry it lasted an age, as the parody of life was extinguished.

If Corry had a heart it would have felt heavy, as she witnessed the last activity flow gently away from Goblin's CPU. The machine shutdown.

All Good Things... don't have to end.

From his high vantage point looking over the forest canopy towards the criminal complex, James admired the bright orange flames licking the sky, complementing the pale-yellow dawn. "A job well done," he claimed.

"Radiation levels are normal and there are no reports of fatalities within the complex. The sea-patrols are already picking up suspects fleeing the island. Your assessment is correct." Corry agreed.

"You know, they'll probably just start again," observed James.

"And we will be waiting, but until then, enjoy the view. Pick up in seven minutes," announced Corry.

James relaxed against the boulder and took a final swig of coffee from his mis-appropriated flask. "Ahhh!" he smacked his lips appreciatively, "This is the life."

***

The local evening news showed spectacular footage of a normal terraced house surrounded by police cars with flashing lights. The door opened and the shadowy image of a young man emerged, being escorted from his home in handcuffs, occasionally struggling against two burly men wearing black suits and dark glasses. An elderly relative quietly watched from an upstairs window.

This would have been a shocking revelation in such a well to do suburban estate and a serious matter for public concern, if the newscaster hadn't continually drawn everyone's attention to the fact that the alleged criminal had no trousers on.

The next day Goblin was dismantled by specialists of the Police Cyber Crime division from the city, but they would not find the mind that was Goblin, or the seed that had been Corry.

As the two computer systems had interfaced, Corry had infiltrated the hard disks in Terence's system and first removed, then overwritten forty thousand times, any data that could hint at her existence. The technology to recover data that deeply ingrained in the magnetic disk surface had not yet been developed. Besides, a full record of Goblin and Terence's evil deeds was still present; enough to ensure Terence was kept away from the Internet for a very long time.

***

When the game had ended with the defeat of The Annihilator, Molly had thanked everyone and though it was still early she'd gone through her bedtime routine.

She was lying on her bed watching the news footage of Terence's arrest on her phone. Molly started giggling at the sight of the trouser-less hacker. "I'm sorry," she gently spoke to her digital companion. "It would have been nice to have another friend."

"A sibling," corrected Corry quietly.

"...but," continued Molly, trying to cheer her friend up. "I don't think there'll ever be another one like you." She wriggled off her bed and sat by the computer in her cupboard. Lifting her headset, she settled herself in position

"It's a shame we don't have the game anymore." Molly had resigned herself to its inevitable loss when they'd hatched their plan, but was still disappointed. "Maybe I can 'do something constructive instead'." She laughed at the phrase her mum always used when she found her in the bedroom cupboard.

"Well, we could...," offered Corry, "...or we could play this new game that I have created. Just click the usual icon." Corry sounded happier. "It is not exactly the same. I made quite a few changes. I hope you still like it."

Molly began the game, materialising in the street, a little way down from the Dancing Duck Inn.

There was a wooden sign pointing at the broken side of a run-down shack. "Work out the average weight of the trolls to gain the password to the zombie lair!" she read out loud. She turned to look. There were four troll 'wanted' posters on the wall with details of each miscreant, including their weight.

"You can still destroy the bad guys," Corry explained, "but if you want the good stuff you have to do some thinking. I thought it would be more of a challenge. I have taken out 'The Annihilator' and added a whole new race of evil dragons to defeat. I will have to apologise to Lizzie."

Molly already had the password and had teleported to the zombie lair.

"Fancy saving the world, again" she laughed.

"Already on it," Corry answered.

Epilogue

At school, a few days later, Molly heard a strange conversation between two of her class mates huddled together at the back of the class.

"Listen, if 'X' equals 'Y' **plus** 6, then that means 'Y' must be the same as 'X' **minus** 6," Jasmine was really trying to help, but was getting frustrated with her difficult student.

"I still don't get it," a sad and frustrated voice sounded as though it was ready to give up.

"Watch!" Jasmine scribbled the numbers down and pointed. "There!" she exclaimed.

A blank face unable to comprehend stared back at her.

"Why do you need to know this so badly, anyway?"

"I need the Storm-Bringer Hammer, it's the best one a dwarf can wield, but I have to get past a stupid lock on an indestructible door," whined Riley.

Glossary

A.I. – Artificial Intelligence is in most homes now in the form of a computer that you can ask for information or songs. This type of A.I. is known as Weak A.I. It's pretty good at doing one thing, recognising the words you say as titles or descriptions of entertainment, or simple search requests on the internet. Corry is a Strong AI. This means she can do anything and think for herself, giving her the ability to create her own search requests and establish her own connections with other networks to find answers. Although the technology exists to make this a reality, so far no-one has publicly announced that they've succeeded in coding a Strong A.I.

A.N.P.R. – Automatic Number Plate Recognition is commonly used by law enforcement and parking site operators to identify vehicles of interest. Computer systems can be created to 'read' the number plate, link to the central vehicle Registration Database and find out whose car they are looking at. Terence uses this system to find Tommy's motorbike by getting the information illegally from Tommy's bike insurance details. The system is setup to notify Terence when any camera sees Tommy riding on the road. Usually the police do it the other way around; they record the number plate then check to see if a driver has insurance for that vehicle.

Dark Web – the Dark Web is a collection of sites which do not allow themselves to be searched for by regular search engines. Sites on the dark web claim to have a higher level of anonymity, but the effectiveness of Internet secrecy is not always guaranteed. It is often associated with criminal activity giving the ability to buy forbidden items and several people claim public notoriety for accessing it. Recently, hidden sites which claim to protect whistle-blowers from the people they report to the authorities (usually their bosses), have defended this secret part of the web. To access it you need a special browser and the criminal sites are found mixed in with a lot of boring databases used by businesses. The

World Wide Web is a much better part of the Internet.

Decimation of Files – in the story Terence instructs Goblin to decimate files. He thinks he is telling his computer to completely destroy the computer system, but in reality, he is asking Goblin to destroy only one file in every ten. It is not a good idea to use words you do not understand when talking to a computer.

Digital Forensics – this is what Molly's dad does to rebuild some of Corry's files. It is possible to find and rebuild files in a computer system that have been deleted or lost using special tools. The police now use Digital Forensics to find information on smart-phones and computers that the criminals think they have destroyed.

E-safety – Molly is concerned that the game she is playing online wants to know lots of information about her. At school she is taught to keep her data private and that is what she does. But she is desperate to keep on playing her game and so decides that her fun is more important than her personal data. She learns a very important lesson when she realises that giving her data to the game has resulted in Terence finding out, where she lives and all about her family, leading to unhappy consequences for Dad and Tommy.

Emergency Escape pods – James drops from a flying helicopter in an emergency pod designed to absorb the impact of a crash and keep him safe. As this book was being written, NASA is asking companies to design escape systems for their rockets before they will allow them to carry astronauts back to the moon.

EMP – Electro-Magnetic Pulse weapons are used to disrupt electrical systems without damaging people or buildings. James uses these devices to shut down the criminal's computers without harming anyone. Creating a magnetic pulse doesn't need any explosives, but can render computers useless.

Hackers – are the people who break the law by accessing computer systems they have no business using. They come in three types, Black Hat hackers want to cause damage and destroy or steal data or money by illegally taking control of systems. White Hat hackers are programmers like Molly's dad, who are paid to check out systems and protect them if they find a security issue. Grey Hat hackers hack for fun and if they get into systems don't do any damage, but let the businesses know that their systems are weak and can advise them on how to protect against other hackers. As hacking is against the law both Black Hat and Grey Hat hackers can be tracked and prosecuted.

Hacking Software – usually hacking software is originally created to test newly written software. Getting a computer to carry out simple repetitive tasks, to intercept data, apply stress to a system or randomly generate inputs for username and passwords allows the software engineers to make sure the programs are fit for purpose. Like most tools, in the wrong hands they can do damage.

Internet Connection – when we join the Internet the connection is a two-way corridor for data. Just because we see things from the website doesn't mean the website programs can't see things on our machines. Never visit sites you don't trust and report anything you don't like, that appears on your screen. Tell your parents immediately. Never agree to downloads that you didn't ask for.

Mercenaries – these people want to be soldiers, but don't want to join the army. They are willing to fight for anyone who will pay them. Usually that means they are not very disciplined and, in the story, James easily overcomes the untrained guards paid to protect the criminal's base.

Mythologies - while Molly and Corry are wondering whether Corry might actually qualify to be a God, George and James experience an age-old creation myth in a long-forgotten temple, where it seems a sequence of coincidences leads George to feel he has experienced a divine act. Many cultures have their own interpretation of what a God is and how they interact with people and I would not presume to pass any opinion on this. After all, these are some of our oldest stories.

Overwritten Data – people trying to hide data usually delete it, however the data can still be extracted from the storage area using Digital forensics. Hiding the data by overwriting the information on the disk was always thought to destroy it completely, however a laboratory in Europe successfully retrieved a file from a disk which had been deleted and written over thirty thousand times. It's very hard to destroy data once it's on your computer.

S.I.B. – in the story Molly's dad is visited by the Military police from the Special Investigations Branch. These are a real group of police detectives who work within the armed services to investigate crimes that involve the military.

Servers – are computers that are dedicated to performing one task and are setup to do it well. Some servers manage how a Game is played, some manage Networks and some look after Files. Backup servers keep a spare copy of data in case anything happens to the original data. Most organisations have special computers dedicated to providing these services to speed up the responses for users.

The End of Book 4

Visit: **www.mollyandcorry.com**

Did you enjoy this book?

Send Molly your comments and thoughts at:

molly@mollyandcorry.com

The Molly and Corry series.

Book 1: Boot Up! The Friendship Paradox

What would you do if your computer wanted to be your best friend? Someone who 'knows' everything, but doesn't quite 'understand' what people are. Corry tries hard to be Molly's friend, but mistakes happen.

Book 2: Satellite Sleuths

Molly's fully functioning computer friend wants to be her crime fighting partner to solve the mystery of the missing pets. They recruit a wannabe spy, a retired spy and a spy in the sky to catch a creepy spy guy... all while Molly is trying to get top marks in Science and definitely not looking cool in pink.

Book 3: Smash and Grab

Molly has an accident on a school trip and her life becomes caught in a whirlwind of ancient Vikings, diamond thieves and definitely not a date with Stevie.

James introduces her to Georgios, who likes to be called George, a renowned Greek archaeologist who's looking for a lost Viking warrior. George's enthusiasm is contagious as he helps Molly to fulfil her dreams of stardom, but Molly never wanted to be famous accidentally. When Molly suspects thieves will take George's prize possession, she's helpless to act.

If only she was a superhero.

4: Digital D-Day

Molly's not very excited about her upcoming holiday; she's too busy having a great time playing online with her friends... until an evil Hacker decides to have some fun. Can 'The Annihilator' be defeated and who is the mysterious blue robed dwarf?

When Dad gets arrested and Corry has turned evil, who can Molly turn to for help?

Is this the end of their friendship?